Wish I Was Here

JACKIE KAY was born in Edinburgh. She is a poet, novelist and writer of short stories and has enjoyed great acclaim for her work for both adults and children. Her novel *Trumpet* won the *Guardian* Fiction Prize, and she has published two collections of stories with Picador, *Why Don't You Stop Talking* and *Wish I Was Here*. Her most recent book is *Red Dust Road*. She teaches at Newcastle University, and lives in Manchester.

JACKIE KAY

WISH I WAS HERE

PICADOR

First published 2006 by Picador

First published in paperback 2007 by Picador

This edition published 2011 by Picador
an imprint of Pan Macmillan, a division of Macmillan Publishers Limited
Pan Macmillan, 20 New Wharf Road, London N1 9RR
Basingstoke and Oxford
Associated companies throughout the world
www.panmacmillan.com

ISBN 978-0-330-51181-0

A CIP catalogue record for this book is available from
the British Library.

Typeset by SetSystems Ltd, Saffron Walden, Essex
Printed in the UK by CPI Mackays, Chatham ME5 8TD

For Julia Darling

Acknowledgements

Some of these stories have been published in *Granta* and the *Guardian*, others were published in *New Writing 2003*, *The Scotsman Orange Anthology* and *The Magic Anthology*.

'What Is Left Behind' was commissioned by the Photographers' Gallery and inspired by the work of J. H. Engstrom.

Others have been broadcast on BBC Radio 3 and 4.

I am very grateful to the Civitelli Ranieri foundation for allowing me to stay in their castle in Italy where I wrote some of these stories.

A big thank you to Maura Dooley, Nick Drake, Catherine Marcangeli, Helen Paris, Ali Smith and Tricia Wood.

Contents

*You go when you can
no longer stay*

It is not so much that we are splitting up that is really worrying me, it is the fact that she keeps quoting Martin Amis. The other day we were in our bedroom having a silly argument about where things hang in the wardrobe when she said to me, 'Like Martin Amis says, you go when you can no longer stay.' It seemed odd to me. I looked outside the window into our street and saw Mr Davies post a letter. I saw three down's white cat walk daintily along our wall, and then jump off. I often say nothing at all when she says something that is perturbing. It seemed odd to me, because here we are two very long-term lesbians, who have been in it so long we look as if we could have knitted each other up, been in it so long we have grown to look the same, wear similar clothes and have almost identical expressions on our plain faces, that Martin Amis should be coming into our lives in this way.

I hadn't even realized she was so keen on him until she made that remark; the one thing we don't share is books. It is the only area of our lives where we are truly different. I read thrillers and human-interest books, about somebody who has done something that I am not likely to do, or somebody who is interested in something that I know nothing about. She reads novels and then she re-reads the novels she has read. And sometimes she reads slim volumes of poetry which always look a little sinister and have very peculiar titles. We are not the kind of couple that share a book, one after the other, which is maybe a shame and maybe if we had been that kind of couple we wouldn't be splitting up now. It seems to me from the amount that she has started quoting Martin Amis that she's had a secret passion for him all along.

We were in the kitchen the other day arguing again about sex. It is a sore point between us. A kind of Achilles heel. 'All marriage turns into a sibling relationship,' she said terrifically confidently. 'Who said that?' I asked with a sickening, sinking heart. She paused, stirring her coffee. 'Do you want a coffee?' she said. 'No, thank you,' I said. 'Don't tell me it was Martin Amis.' 'Yes,' she said defensively. 'He's quite right. You just don't fancy each other after a while.'

'I fancy you,' I said, then instantly regretted it.

'No you don't, you think you do,' she said, adding a big splash of milk into the coffee mug. 'Sure you don't want a cup?' she said. 'All right, then,' I said. And she quite gleefully got another mug out of the kitchen cupboard. I think I bought the mug but I can't be sure. She smiled at me. When she smiles at me, I remember who she is. Then she said, 'You become far too similar, especially two women. It's like looking in the mirror. You need a bit of difference to feel real passion.' 'Oh,' I said and sipped at my coffee anxiously. 'Life is too short not to feel passion,' she said. I knew where it was all going, but I didn't want her to tell me. I actually wanted to hide. I wanted to run up the stairs and hide in the airing cupboard. I couldn't stop thinking about my eighty-two-year-old mother, who was even fonder of Hilary than she was of me, who had taken years to accept our relationship and then had finally totally embraced it. My old mother would be devastated. I felt edgy just thinking about it.

'Do you want a Jaffa with your coffee?' she asked me, as if a Jaffa could be the answer to all my troubles, as if a Jaffa could truly console. 'Yes, please,' I said. I'd got into the habit of saying yes to as many things as possible, thinking that if I said yes enough she might stop saying no. She put three Jaffas on my plate but I noticed she took none for herself. 'Aren't you having any?' I asked her, a bit alarmed. 'No,' she said. 'Why not?' I said. 'Oh, for goodness' sake, Ruth, stop trying to control me. After a while all relationships turn into power struggles,' she said. 'Would you ask that same question to a friend?'

'I'm just wondering why you put three on a plate for me if you're not having any yourself,' I said suspiciously. I was becoming very suspicious of her because she had started to change all of her habits and it was very worrying to me. 'Do you know something?' she said, very nastily. 'I think you are going mad.'

'Does Martin Amis say that?' I said furiously. 'Does he say one person in a couple during a break-up will always accuse the other of going mad?'

She sighed and shook her head. She was actually looking quite beautiful these days. The person I didn't want to hear about was clearly making her feel good about herself. 'I'm just trying to have a cup of coffee with you, that's all. If I can't have a cup of coffee with you without fighting, we will have to put the house on the market even sooner than we said. As Martin Amis says, you go when you can no longer stay,' she said, standing up in the kitchen and drinking her coffee. She wouldn't sit down these days. There it was again, that bloody awful quote. It was deliberate then. She knew it was agitating me; she'd started to repeat it at random in whatever corner of our house we found ourselves in. I could even hear it in my sleep.

She left the room, coffee in hand, and I heard her playing music up the stairs. She'd taken to playing music a lot recently, another big change for her. This was a thin voice I didn't much like, one of those new English jazz singers with a very insipid style. I preferred the Dinah Washingtons of this world. I got up from the table and put two of the Jaffa cakes in the bin. I gave the third to our dog. I saw what she was up to. She was trying to fatten me up as she lost weight. Well, we were both a little on the generous side. I was about three stone overweight and Hilary was at least two. Whenever we went out to a big lesbian do, I noticed that we weren't the only long-term couple that was overweight. I used to think that was happiness, being fat together, rolling about from one side of the big double bed to the other. Most of our old relationship revolved around food. Our idea of a super day used to be a day when we were both off work. (Now I notice her days off don't coincide with mine any more.) Hilary didn't have to go into the council, which was depressing her, and I didn't have to go into the tax office, which was depressing me. We'd get into our big bed with lots of treats – a couple of Chow Mein Pot Noodles, a big plate of chocolate biscuits, a big pot of cookies-and-cream Häagen-Dazs. Bliss. And we'd watch *The Maltese Falcon* for the umpteenth time or *Now, Voyager* or *All About Eve*. Heaven. A day like that was even nicer if it was raining outside. At the end of *Now, Voyager*, we'd both say that line together, 'Oh, Jerry, don't let's ask for the moon, we have the stars,' and clutch at each other as if we were frightened of losing everything.

A lot of the people who know us often get us mixed up as though we were identical twins. Some people call me Hilary and Hilary Ruth. It's a bit silly because we don't really look all that alike. Admittedly we do both buy similar-looking clothes in Marks and Spencer. Our casual-clothes days and smart-clothes days are always the same. But recently Hilary has started to shop in Harvey Nichols. I went in there one day on my own and took a look at some of the prices. They actually made me feel quite ill and I felt terribly worried. That night I said to Hilary, 'I don't think shopping at Harvey Nichols on your salary is very sensible.' She was reading the new Martin Amis at the time, *Yellow Dog*. 'This is about a man who suddenly becomes very violent,' she said quite menacingly. I said, 'I feel as if I'm living with a gambler. You have run up massive bills on our joint Visa.'

'I told you we should never have had a joint account,' Hilary said and got up and opened a bottle of red wine, which was another curious thing, because we only usually have a nice bottle of white, a Chardonnay, at the weekend. Now Hilary has taken to red wines, big heavy reds like Cabernet Sauvignons and Riojas and she's taken to drinking them during the week. She slurped her wine. I noticed that she'd lost quite a bit of weight. 'Anyway, I think you should be a bit more careful,' I said, trying to sound calm. 'I think you should stop being a control freak,' she said. Then she got up and left the room again, taking her glass and the bottle with her. I heard the music go on up the stairs. She was playing it really quite loud. This time it was Otis Redding. We haven't played Otis Redding for years. She came running back down the stairs. I thought she was going to apologize, but she just picked up *Yellow Dog* without a word and went back upstairs. I could hear Otis singing 'Sitting on the Dock of the Bay'.

I was annoyed at myself. I started clearing away the remains of our meal. I noticed that Hilary had left all of her rice. She'd eaten her salad, though. I didn't know quite what to do with myself because we usually watched *Frost* on the TV together or *Miss Marple* or *Midsomer Murders*. But lately Hilary had said, 'That isn't me, watching *Frost*. That's you.' She'd started saying this a lot recently. 'I'm not the kind of person who does such and such or who says such and such or who watches such and such.' I wondered furiously if Martin Amis had put her up to that too. Perhaps there was something in one of his books that advised people in long-term relationships to stop doing everything that they used to enjoy doing. Perhaps he, being so resolutely heterosexual, so smug with his roll-ups, was trying to destroy the lesbian relationship. I suddenly had a brainwave. If she was reading him, the only thing I could do to read her was read him too. I rushed into Waterstone's in town and bought everything they had by him. I hid the books under the spare-room bed, the spare room which I have now been consigned to. Hilary needs space to think about what we should do, she has said. She needs space and calm. I have stopped reading my murder mysteries for the moment. Hilary always looked down upon them. Of course she thinks she is much cleverer than me. 'It's always the woman that gets it,' she'd say whenever I picked up another thriller.

I've started to feel very odd within my own life. It's most peculiar to feel lonely inside your own life. It's a secret, of course, because nobody would know and all of our friends still think everything is fine between us, though I must say they have all taken to admiring Hilary recently and saying things like, 'You're looking great.' This morning we had breakfast together, which was a nice change. Sunday breakfast. Hilary had bacon and egg but no toast and no newspapers. She has even given up the Sunday papers; I'm not sure why. When I asked her about it, she said, 'Do I have to explain everything to you?' Then when she saw my slightly hurt face, she said, 'I'm engrossed in *Yellow Dog* and newspapers are a huge waste of time.'

I suggested we go out for a Sunday walk or a run in the car in the afternoon. Hilary said yes, good idea. I felt very pleased about this because it seemed to me that if we could go out for a walk in some beautiful countryside normal life might return, encouraged by the light on the hills or a gushing waterfall. 'Shall we go to Coniston Water or Derwent Water and then go for Sunday lunch in a pub somewhere?' I said excitedly. 'No, I don't want to make a big production out of it,' Hilary said. 'Let's just go to the park with Orlando. I've got other things I want to do today.' The dog was wagging her tail as Hilary fetched the lead, wagging her tail frantically.

It was a freezing-cold day. I had my scarf tied firmly around my neck. Hilary looked a bit bare but I daren't suggest she put a scarf on. I rather like the winter cold if I am well wrapped up. We were walking side by side, with our dog Orlando running on happily in front of us, when Hilary suddenly said to me, 'I thought it best that we talk about this outside of the house rather than in. You know I have not been happy for some time.'

'I didn't know that,' I said, hurt.

'Oh, come on. You did, darling,' Hilary said, quite gently. I shook my head and put my hands in my pockets. Our dog ran back towards us. I picked up her stick and threw it again really quite far. It was truly an astonishingly beautiful winter day; even the clouds were lit up from behind as if they had highlights in their hair. 'Isn't it lovely light today?' I said. 'Isn't it absolutely gorgeous?'

'Why won't you let me talk about this?' Hilary said.

'Don't spoil our walk, darling,' I said, picking up the stick again and throwing it. It was the coldest it had been yet. Freezing bitter cold, but still very beautiful, beautiful in an icy, frosty way. The ducks and the geese were sitting on top of the ice on the pond as if they were on holiday. Hilary sighed beside me. I could tell she was about to try again. 'I know that you are finding this hard, that's only natural. I know that we thought we'd be together forever. But stuff happens; life changes. We have to move on.'

I walked beside her. At least she hadn't quoted again from Martin Amis, nor had she told me her name. I presumed it was a she, anyway. I didn't want to know her name; I didn't want to know what she looked like; I didn't want to know anything about her. 'Could you at least do me one favour?' I asked Hilary. 'Could you tell me nothing about her, nothing at all?'

'That's silly,' Hilary said. 'I'm not buying into that. I've done nothing to be ashamed of.'

'You've stopped loving me,' I said, quietly.

'We weren't good for each other any more,' she said. I looked at her and suddenly noticed that she'd lost at least three stone. 'How have you lost all this weight?' I asked her. 'I don't want to tell you,' she said. 'I don't want you copying that too. You copy everything. If you hadn't copied everything, we might still have been lovers.'

'What do I copy?' I said, feeling extremely alarmed.

'Nothing,' she said. 'Never mind.' We walked round the pond in silence. I noted a few things I think about the geese but I can't remember what they were.

I noticed that Hilary was sweating quite profusely even though it was sub-zero temperatures. I sneaked a look at her. She had that mad look on her face, eyebrows knitted together, quite unappealing if I am honest. It occurred to me that she might be having her menopause and that all of these changes of behaviour were actually the change of life. She had after all been behaving very erratically recently, flying off the handle at the slightest thing. 'Are you having a hot flush?' I asked her.

'No I certainly am not!' she said.

But it was out and now I knew. Hilary was having her menopause and keeping it secret from me. That explained everything: it explained why she no longer wanted to share the double bed. The sheets were probably soaking in the middle of the night! It explained the temper tantrums and the outbursts. 'Why didn't you just tell me? For goodness' sake, we are both lesbians,' I said. 'You might describe yourself like that. You know I don't,' she said. 'Well, whatever, why didn't you tell me you were having hot flushes?' Hilary is three years younger than I am and I could tell she was fuming, absolutely fuming, about getting her change of life first. 'It can happen at any age,' I said. 'I've just been lucky I haven't had mine yet. I was a late starter with my periods. When you start late, you apparently have your menopause later. Did you start yours early?'

'Don't do this.' Hilary was beside herself now. 'I am not having my menopause. I don't know how many times I have to say this,' she said, tired. 'This is typical of you. You are in denial. I am in love. This is a love story of all the strange things happening to me so late in the goddamned day.' She wasn't going to get me this time with that Martin Amis. I said, 'When I come in the door I go tee hee hee. The place kills me.'

She said, 'Have you been reading him?'

'Yes,' I said, quite pleased.

'See, I told you, you always had to copy me,' she said, apoplectic with rage now. 'And now you've gone out and bought him. Nothing's sacred.'

I smiled. I shouted, '*Or-lan-do*,' my voice going up and down merrily. 'Who is going to have the dog?' I said. 'I am,' Hilary said. 'I'm much fonder of Orlando than you are. Orlando is my dog.'

'She is not,' I said indignantly.

'I don't think I want to do this,' Hilary said.

'Do what?' I said, still like a fool feeling a little hopeful.

'Have these silly fights. We are two grown-ups. We have to be able to sort this out amicably. It's not like we have kids.'

'Having a dog is like having a kid,' I said.

'It is not. Don't be stupid.'

We walked in silence then round the pond for the third time. I couldn't count the amount of times we have walked round and round and round that pond. I thought of all the walks over our twenty-five years together. Our walking books are the only books we truly share, tiny leaflet-sized books that tell us of lengths and grades of difficulty in Strathglass and surrounding glens. I thought of our favourite walk from just below Beinn Mhor, and the lovely waterfall in the woods up the hill from the old sheep fanks. And the odd little cemetery you come across as you reach the end of the walk. Rumour has it that once a burial party arrived there from Tomich village minus the coffin. I thought of all the walks over all the years – off the beaten track and out of breath. Parts of the country, we used to believe, truly belonged to us: the Lakes, the Highlands, the Peak District. I couldn't bear to think of Hilary anywhere, in any of these places with some other love, her dark fleece zipped up, her walking boots thick with mud, and a map in her hand. I looked at Hilary. I couldn't imagine her even wearing a fleece in the future. She looked so slim now; she looked like somebody else, oddly focused and deliberate-looking as if the resolve to do this had made her quite certain of herself. I couldn't quite believe it. Hilary had slimmed her way out of my hands. When we got inside our cream kitchen, I thought she might have a cup of tea and a scone and jam for old times' sake. 'Scones are a thing of the past,' Hilary said and I had the impression that she wasn't quoting from Martin Amis this time.

It seemed to me that Hilary wanted to consign our whole life to the past. The other day I arrived home, very excited, with a classic copy of the *Dandy* – December the 30th, 1972. Hilary and I have collected comics for over ten years and have spent many a happy hour laughing over the antics of Dennis the Menace or Desperate Dan or Beryl the Peril. I said triumphantly, 'Look what I've just found!' thinking that Hilary would remember our love through Beryl the Peril's impersonation of an Abominable Snowman. But Hilary just stared at it a little disdainfully and said, 'You can have the comic collection, that was always more your thing. I'll have the CDs.'

I put the kettle on and got out a fresh jar of rhubarb-and-ginger jam. I pulled the little bit of tracing paper off the top. I opened our cake tin and took out one of yesterday's homemade scones, a nice batch that had risen properly. I buttered my scone quite thickly and spread the nippy jam over it. I made a fresh pot of tea and put the cosy on. I sat down alone at the table. I poured us both a mug of tea. Hilary watched me eat my scone with some satisfaction, sipping at her mug of tea, standing, leaning against the fridge. She said nothing. She eyed me eating my scone. I wasn't the least bit bothered. I thought ahead to night-time in the spare room. I said to myself secretly another Martin Amis line: 'Jesus Christ, if I could make it into bed and get my eyes shut without seeing a mirror.' She smiled at me and I smiled back at her and both of our faces looked the same. We both had his tight, cool grin.

What is left behind

We left the room behind ourselves. We were always leaving rooms behind, going back to our lives. The morning when we got into our cars to drive away from our small piece of something was always bleak. I couldn't see proper. We never could afford a suite or anything like that but still it was our room for one night and in a couple of weeks we might get away from our lives again to have another night and then we'd be back on the freeway. I'd drive my car in the opposite direction, back to my blurred house with the hazy tree outside. I don't know how many rooms we've had, must be a lot in four years. I never go in and say, Oh, look, isn't this a nice room? No, I don't recall ever doing that. Those rooms always have something of other people in them, somebody's hair left on the pillow.

We're thinking: We have this room and we have it for this night and we have our naked bodies. We got everything so pared down. Before our rooms, my body was like a gone thing. Sure, I used it. I got up and I moved around the house and got in the car; but I didn't really know it. It was real slow. Until we got the rooms, and then my body was suddenly there in the room. We would look at ourselves in those smudged mirrors, and I'd see my breasts, I'd see their round shapes for the first time in years. I'd see my belly, how soft it seemed.

We mostly didn't get much sleep and those rooms never got properly dark anyhow. There was always some light coming in from outside. The walls are thinner in motels than they are just about anywhere. You can hear other couples getting up to what you are getting up to and that's not nice. You don't like to think of yourself the same as other people in that respect. Every room we left in that time would stay in my head afterwards. We always left the bed unmade in a heap of blankets and sheets with bare bits of mattress exposed like the bed could still hold us when we couldn't hold each other no more. I'd be driving home in the driving rain and I'd be thinking about the unmade bed we left, wishing a bed could pull you back, a bed could make demands, a bed could say you can't just up and leave like that.

Those nights in those motel rooms I was messier than I'd ever been in my whole life. We drank straight from bottles of beer and fell asleep for two hours maybe after the dawn fogged in – the kind of sleep where you don't know whose body is whose and the sweat from your sex is on you and you are naked underneath your sheets and your dream is her dream and her dream is yours and you can't tell if you are properly asleep. We'd wake up and I'd take a look at her face and I wouldn't be able to believe my eyes. Her face was all soft and smudged-looking, like some of her definition had been rubbed away in the night; we both looked like that, I guess. Like we didn't have any hard lines any more, like somebody had drawn us with a soft pencil, like we could be rubbed out. We'd stare and stare until we'd fill up again and want more. I couldn't imagine not wanting to suck her nipple, to touch the crack of her ass, to run my hand down the length of her back, to ride her like I used to ride a bare-backed horse out west. Then one of us would say the horrible words. She'd say, We have to be getting along now. And I'd say, Just two more minutes, and she'd sigh and say, We have to be getting back or we're going to arouse suspicions. I'd say, Don't talk about arousing suspicions. And she'd say, You know what I mean. Then we got up and she'd shower faster than me and I'd shower slower than her and somehow we both got dried. I'd put on my clean pants while she watched. It didn't take all that long. Soon as I was dressed, it all felt changed already. I was bereft and wanting bed again.

When I was back in my other life without her, I'd think about her in my head all day, about how her body looked in one room after another. How straight-forward she was with her naked body, how she just sat naked like somebody would sit clothed. She was never shy or coy. It was like, here are my breasts, here's my pubic hair. Here's what there is to me – take what you like till tomorrow; then I'm gone. It was simple – as far as anything complicated is simple – simple, because

I loved her. I'd be back in my life with my man and he'd be watching *Pimp My Ride* and I'd be thinking of getting back to the room. He'd say, What are you thinking about? I'm not thinking about anything much, I'd say. You got that faraway look again, he'd say. I'd go upstairs and try and wash the faraway look from my face. And that night in bed I'd pleasure him. I'd lie there and think of the rooms, the unmade bed, the sheets the way they looked unfurled, the way they lost themselves, the way they looked shaken up, the way they made ghost shapes of us. He'd pat my back and say, Good girl. Good girl. And I'd say, Good night, hon. Then I'd lie there and dream about those rooms in my life, one after the other, Room 55, Room 711, Room 401, Room 404, Room 161, room with pink candlewick bedspread. Room with big fat radiator, room with sheet of plastic on the divan, room with dark wood panelling, room with twin beds pushed together, room with puke-yellow bathroom, room with baby-blue blanket. Did I love those bleak rooms! I'd lie and recite them and try and get the order right, when we stayed in Room 711 – was that before Room 1526? It was too. Room 99. Room 491. Room 22. Come in. Room, Room, Room. Oh room. Oh God. Please. Oh my Room 55. Room with the broken curtain rail. Oh, please. Room with vulgar wallpaper. Don't stop. Room with the elaborate Privacy sign.

Two weeks go by somehow. It's true what they say about time when you look forward too much. I only

live in the moment now when I am with my girl.
Otherwise I'm looking forward or back. Finally time
gets round to Tuesday. I drive off to meet her. I get to
Room 301 first. I have a smudge of lipstick on and I'm
wearing my new jeans. She is always punctual, but I
am always early. I sit on the edge of the armchair next
to the bed. There's a cream phone in this room, a thin
green carpet, a painting of a church in the snow. I
imagine us talking fast and hot into each other's ears.
I imagine us on the bed opposite. I look at my watch.
After four weeks' waiting, you'd think ten minutes
wouldn't be long. Ten minutes late, then fifteen. Then
thirty. I take off my clothes and get under the covers.
Two hours late. I start to moan. I get up naked and sit
on the chair again, wrapping the blanket round myself.
I stare at the door. Four hours late. I get back into
bed, under the sheets. Room 704. Room 711. Room
55. Room 1521. Room 408. Room 1526. Room with
painting of a church in the snow. I feel myself slide
under. My skin slips down beneath the covers. My skin
meets the white sheet. My body takes leave of itself.
My body leaves my skin behind. My skin, sheets. I try
and think how her voice sounds exactly. I try and get
it right. I have her say something to me. I have her say,
Remember you always wanted to be the bed after we
had left the room. I don't remember that, I have myself
say. I don't remember ever wanting that. You did, I
have her say, kissing the air in the room that used to
be my face. I don't think I ever wanted that I say as the

tears that used to be on my face dampen the air in the room till the room tastes of the sea, the misty sea, close to the big Atlantic. Remember how you always wanted to drive to the ocean, I have her say. You always wanted to get in my car and drive away. You wanted to go someplace in the country and cut up our own logs and build our own fire. Remember that? No, I say, tossing my hair now so that the covers in the room shake on their own, flapping up and down creating enough wind for a storm, a big storm on a dark night. No, I say, shaking like the tree outside the motel room is shaking, so hard the branches are indistinct from one another, no, I say as all the feathers from the pillow fly around the room like snowflakes. No, I don't remember that. I don't remember nothing. I don't have all that many memories.

Wish I was here

They will be flying in today, the day after me, thumping down on the runway. If the flights are on time, they should get here around four. I'll be a nice surprise for them. It's bound to be a bit boring: two lovers on their own for two whole weeks; when they run out of things to say, I'll be here to chip in. I've been told I'm good company. I've been told that twice in my life and each time it has gone in.

But they're coming with a different holiday company from mine – more upmarket. At least they won't be met by *Syooozie* from *Liverpyooool*. And they won't be coming to this hotel. Lucky them! They will be staying at the hotel that I can see from my tiny balcony, the Princess Hotel, 'Gooda die, madam, how arra you?' It's a five-star hotel with strangely white sand and shiny green grass and symmetrical palm trees. It does have a bit of authentic beach at the south end of the hotel leading to the genuine sea. Must be a shock for those residents, the sea, the totally real sea. It can drown people; it doesn't compromise; sometimes the red flag goes up which means people really shouldn't swim. There are slobs and yobs that always ignore this and

27

roar into the waves, slipping and sliding and yelling their heads off. People who are not residents of the Princess Hotel are not supposed to hang out on that bit of private beach, but yesterday I found it quite simple to bluff my way in and look like somebody who stays in a five-star hotel – which nowadays is like nothing at all because everybody is so casual. Even the rich are casual these days, more laid-back than ever. Frauds. I swam along from where my hotel is and lay down on one of their sunbeds. I peeled off my skin-tight bathing cap and tossed it onto a sunbed to bag the bed; any little polite sign is enough at these private places to claim a space. Then I returned to my bit of beach, and grabbed my stuff hurrying back to the sunbed with the swimming cap. It was a bit complicated, but it worked.

Anyway their beach is cleaner and quieter and why should places be exclusive to people who pay money? Why should their sunbeds be free when they are the ones who are loaded? You have to pay a lot of euros for a sunbed on the ordinary beach; it's a rip-off and you might not be there all day. Me, I'd end up lying there till the sun sizzled into the sea, until I was well and truly fried, just to get my money's worth. I've got a head start over them anyway and am getting darker by the minute. There's nobody to rub the sun-tan cream into my back yet but that will soon change. Their plane will be touching down very, very soon.

I've spent the day swimming and reading and snoozing in the sun and when the sun has become too hot for me I've dragged my sunbed into the shade. I dreamt a bit and when I woke up I felt embarrassed that I'd been dreaming in a public place. Every year I take a classic and a book recommended by a friend because I don't read enough to keep up with what is going on. This year I've got *Villette*, because I've read *Wuthering Heights*, but not *Villette*. It's got some oil on it already, which will at least prove I started it.

Everybody here is with somebody else except me. Everybody in the whole wide world is in a couple or part of a family or with a bunch of friends. Some people are playing volleyball and some playing bat and ball and some kids are making very elaborate castles, with moats and stuff. I wouldn't mind helping to build a castle or having a game of something, but you look weird these days – a lone adult who wants to play with children. The most you can do is smile and even that feels slightly iffy. *Wot's she grinning at, then?* Last night at dinner, I sat at a table for one in my hotel – *para uno, para uno, uno, uno*, I said till I was understood – because I didn't want to go out on my own. When I was choosing from some of the wide selection of salads at the buffet, a thin woman whom I'd noticed sitting at the next table to mine with a very overweight husband said to me, 'Great selection of salads, isn't it?' and I felt stupidly grateful that someone was talking to me. The extra-large husband was digging into a huge portion of kleftiko. 'It is,' I said, 'wonderful. Salad's good for you.' I was just about to say something else about the food when she moved on. I put an extra couple of slices of big tomatoes on my plate with some cubes of feta, a few olives and a portion of swordfish and sat back down at my table for one. I started eating fish again eight years ago. I began with the tiddlers and the whitebait and sardines and have finally worked my way up to swordfish, a really meaty fish. The woman sitting across from me smiled as I dropped my olive stone onto a tea plate. I think she felt sorry for me being on my own. I opened my *Villette* to see what she was up to.

I'm glad I chose to eat here for my first night and I don't suppose we'll be eating in the hotel much. We're more likely to go and find some non-touristy tavernas up in the hills. I hope they haven't booked half-board. No! Claudette always said she'd be bored by half-board.

It gets very suddenly dark here; the dark just comes down like somebody with two great big fists in the sky yanking down the roller blinds. Claudette and I had been going on holidays together for five years before Claudette met New Lover. I thought New Lover wouldn't last beyond the holiday booking and that Claudette would get rid of her and take me, maybe having to pay a bit extra for the change of plan. But when it seemed as if everything was still going well between them – why, I don't know, can't work it out, they seem completely unsuited – I decided to book myself. I know Claudette will be glad of my company when she gets here because she's told me many times in the past decade that I am her favourite person to go on holiday with. Both Claudette and I have been lover-less for many years. With me it is exactly ten, with Claudette about four or five until Jan appeared on the scene. When two women are best friends and both are single, it's a real blow when one of them finds a lover. Don't get me wrong; I'm happy for Claudette, just bloody miserable for myself. I mean it almost feels as if she has cheated on me and dumped me in Club Undesirable all on my own. All that talk about being unattractive and feeling fat, and finding the weight harder to shift; all that talk of getting old and boring and saying staying in is the new going out, just to suddenly swoop round one day to my house with New Lover. And not to have warned me properly! Not to have prepared me for it!

I'd never seen that look on Claudette's face before, her colour darker with it, the passion, she was practic-ally frothing at the mouth and she looked even more beautiful than I'd ever seen her look. But Jan is a bit dull: the clothes are a total mess, the hair's a mess. It's unbelievable. I said to Claudette when she left, 'Erm, what is she doing with her hair?' To be fair, Jan is one of those people who can wear any old thing and still look kind of attractive, one of those people that gets her hair done deliberately to look as if she's just got out of bed. But the biggest thing that is striking about Jan is that she is nine years younger than Claudette, which makes her fourteen years younger than me. It is so unfair that Claudette should net a catch quicker than me because I've been longer without a lover than her and I've been keeping myself trim and she hasn't. I watch what I eat. I avoid carbohydrates after midday like the plague. I watch how much I drink – except of course on holiday. Claudette drinks like a fish. I cook all fresh food for myself and lay out some beautiful little dinners to have with the TV, and I don't eat any of those microwave meals. I don't have a microwave. I do have a mobile phone because I liked the idea of little texts like little love letters, though so far I haven't had many texts, but maybe it takes a while to build up contacts. To tell you the truth, I can't imagine ever having a lover again. The last lover I had left me on the stroke of midnight at New Year's ten years ago. She told me it was her New Year's resolution to go celibate for a period which I broken-heartedly accepted until I saw her snogging somebody else on January the fifth. I can't imagine anybody touching my body ever again. My body feels lonely, only comfortable with me, like an old dog that barks at strangers. I'm not even that old – I'm forty-four for goodness' sake – but I feel old because I haven't got a lover. It's harder to meet new people at my age. *Aw poor Paula boo-boos.*

Claudette and I have had some amazing holidays in the past. Once we almost slept together and then decided it would be the end of a major friendship because sleeping with friends always goes wrong, so we had another glass of retsina, which I forced myself to down because Claudette loves the stuff, and a bit of a long-ish kiss and then went to our separate beds. Mine was very hard. I didn't sleep for hours. I tossed and turned with my heart racing in the dark. Another time we went camping on the Isle of Mull, which was a great holiday too and would have been perfect if it wasn't for the midges. A midge bit me. My leg doubled its size and I had to be driven to the community hospital, Dunaros, from Calgary to Salen in the middle of our holiday in the middle of the night. The smell of ferns in the rain was nice, though. The Mull doctor told me in his lovely Highland-Island accent that a 'rogue midge' had probably bitten me. A 'rogue midge that haes swallad a wee bit o' coo dung ur horse minooor and deposited it in yir leg, dearie.' Great, I thought, a *rogue midge*! Claudette wasn't all that sympathetic. When she came to visit me in hospital, she said, 'You always get ill on holidays.' Tell me about it – the bad Venice oyster, the Lake Garda shower mat. We ended up at a hospital in the hills that time. There was a beautiful view up there and I said to Claudette, 'Just think, we wouldn't have got to see this beautiful view if it hadn't been for me falling and breaking my wrist.' I can't remember what Claudette said to that. I think she agreed and smiled at me affectionately.

Although I'm forty-four, people think that I am quite a bit younger. My friends think that I dress very young. I like wearing short skirts and sporty tops. Because I'm quite trim and small in height, I get a lot of my clothes at Gap Kids, which means I save a lot of money. I like their stuff. Well, I'm not loaded, not like Jan, who clearly has a big wad to throw around – not in my direction, more's the pity. She bought Claudette a turquoise iMac, a bit OTT when you've only been dating a couple of months. She bought one of those PlayStation 2 things to play with round at Claudette's. She spends hours doing those violent games. Excuse me? She's tall and her hair hangs over her face and she's got very well-defined cheekbones. But not a lot going on upstairs, it seems to me.

I look at my watch. It is four thirty. I must have fallen off to sleep reading *Villette*. The book is lying open across my stomach. I am dribbling a little. I wipe my mouth. I'm hungry, but I won't eat anything for now. I don't want to go back to my hotel in case I miss them. They are bound to come out soon to explore and get their bearings. Claudette and I always just dumped our bags and went straight out to investigate. I scan the beach for Claudette. She is so familiar; I'd spot her right away. Every time I see somebody that I think is her, my heart skips. You'd think I didn't see her all the time, but something about meeting somebody you know in a foreign place is so exciting.

There's a tall good-looking man drying in between his legs with a pale orange hotel towel. There's a small boy sleeping with a T-shirt covering his head. There's a family playing rounders and arguing about who is out. Next to me is a boy with red hair who looks like he is in for bad sunburn, lying asleep on his sunbed with his Discman on. I wonder whether or not to shake the young man awake – his parents have left him for the moment – and tell him he's going to be in a lot of pain tomorrow. I shouldn't care what people would think, only about doing somebody a favour. I shake him awake and I say, 'I think you're going to be in a lot of pain tomorrow if you stay out in the sun.' He looks at me for quite a while, a bit dozy and vacant and he turns round on his other side and falls asleep again.

I look towards the Princess Hotel's pathway with the palm trees and the bougainvillaea out in bloom and all the other bright flowers; Claudette would know their names. She is good on flowers and I am good on birds. I once got Claudette to come birdwatching with me in Wales and I wept when I saw baby red kites swoop from their nest and spin in the sky. It was the most beautiful thing I ever saw. Claudette hugged me that time and said, 'You're so sensitive, aren't you?' I smiled through my tears.

I look up again. I think I will pack up my things and go to their bar and have a drink. Anybody can have a drink in there, not just the residents. We were all supposed to be going on holiday together when Claudette told me that Jan had said they should treat themselves: five-star hotel, heated pool, games room, mini-bar, satellite TV, yuk. I couldn't afford that kind of money; it was way, way too expensive for me, so I said so. I expected Claudette to back down and say that we would all go to the hotel I could afford, a two-star, which in a way seemed a lot nicer, but she didn't. So I said I wasn't coming at all. And she just said, 'Never mind, another time, Paula. We've had loads of holidays over the years and we'll have loads more to come.' We used to send postcards to friends. Claudette would put Paula sends her love on hers and I would put Claudette sends her love on mine, but I won't be able to do that now. Jan will write the postcards now, from both of them, to people I don't even know.

When I said to Claudette, 'I'm not being funny but you two seem so different, what's the big attraction?' Claudette told me that Jan is dynamite in bed. I must say I hated that expression and it sounded not like Claudette at all, more like Jan's way of speaking. Claudette has started saying things that I would never have believed she would say in a month of Sundays. Like she said that her new haircut was *minging*, because Jan says the word *minging* all the time. I almost threw up. I walked stiffly to the toilet and I felt the saliva gathering in my mouth but I managed to swallow it down. She's right, my Claudette, I am sensitive.

Not long after I arrived yesterday, I went to check out their hotel. But I didn't like it – impersonal, no character. All marble corridors and huge reception desk. There was plenty to do if you had kids – ping-pong tables, pool tables, a kiddie club that kept shouting announcements over the hotel's loudspeaker every half-hour, 'Yes, it's water-polo time in the heated pool at the Princess Hotel' – enough to drive you crazy. They won't get much peace here, I thought, we'll have to find other nice, quiet places to go. I've bought a map and I know that Jan can drive and is cool about driving abroad, so Claudette tells me and I hope that is right because I am a nervous passenger even in my own country. Anyway that's one benefit in having her here: she can do the driving. I've even looked into car-hire prices and if we picked a small car, we could get a reasonable deal.

The other thing I did while I was over in their hotel yesterday was something I've never had done before in my life. I went for a manicure. The woman told me I needed to moisturize my cuticles and that I should use anti-ageing cream on my hands. She spoke good English with a very strong accent. 'Your face, well you can lift your face, you can give it a facelift, no? Your bottom, you can get liposuction, but your hands, when your hands age, there is nothing to do, there is no going back. Start using this anti-ageing cream from thirty-three at the very latest; this is emergency.' I was so flattered that she thought I was under thirty-three that I bought the thirty-euro cream. A huge extravagance for me. I felt quite ill after it, dizzy with my own recklessness. The cream plus the manicure had set me back fifty euros. I'd only brought three hundred for the two weeks. I'd need to scrounge some money from Claudette or Jan. The cream came with soft white gloves. 'Put them on at night, put your hands in the gloves and go to sleep.' It is the kind of thing you can do when you don't have a lover. I wore the gloves last night and had a horrible dream about Jan. She had used my white gloves for gardening and they were covered in mud. I actually woke myself up shrieking, 'They are obviously not gardening gloves! Any fool can see that!' I was so loud I worried that the couple in the room next door might have heard me. But I don't know why I bothered because it took me ages to get to sleep with all the commotion and people running up and down the corridors screaming and laughing. Coming to places like this in peak season is a living hell.

I am sitting in their hotel bar. It is five o'clock. 'Eet eees happy hour, happy hour at the Preencess Hotel,' a thin voice announces from the loud speaker. 'Two dreenks for the price of a-one.' I don't actually want two drinks. But when I asked the bartender if I could get my one drink half-priced, he didn't seem to under-stand what I was saying. So I took the two gins and tonics and I'm now feeling a bit tipsy because I'm not used to drinking during the day and the sun has gone to my head. I feel like giggling but I can't sit here and giggle to myself. I'm a bit underdressed in my Gap shorts and V-necked T-shirt. I should really have gone back to my hotel and got changed. But I didn't want to miss them. It occurred to me that maybe they would want their first night to themselves, and then I thought, No, they will have had all that time on the aeroplane, that's about four hours, that's plenty.

By the time the pair of them turn up at the bar, I'm on my fourth G&T and am feeling in a real holiday mood. I wouldn't mind dancing. They don't see me. They are both dressed in light-coloured clothes, though Claudette is wearing a linen dress I haven't seen her in, must be new for the holiday, and Jan is wearing white linen trousers and a white shirt. She looks the smartest I've seen her. I feel even more self-conscious that I'm just wearing my clothes from the beach, so I think I will sneak out and get changed and come back. I worry that they might catch a glimpse of me, but they are totally engrossed in each other and are lightly touching each other's hands. I can almost feel it from where I am standing. It burns like the boy's back will burn tomorrow.

I rush back to my small room, which smells faintly of bad sewage, bad sewage smells of cabbage, cabbages are people without lovers. I feel really discontent and a bit drunk. I should have splashed out and stayed over there after all. I put on my new jeans, even though they will be a bit hot, because I look good in them and a new designer top that I got for my last birthday. I put on a tiny bit of lipstick. It smudges. It's actually quite hard to do your lips when you are tipsy. My face has had a right blast of the sun so I look not bad.

I walk back from my hotel to their hotel, singing to myself a song I sang years ago in a jazz-dancing class in school and it has just come into my head for no reason except that I saw a woman who looked a bit like the teacher and I used to love that teacher. She was my first crush. 'Sonny, yesterday my life was full of tears ... Sonny, once so true, I love you. Sonny, once so true, I love you-ooo.' I remember the moves that went with the song and I start doing them on the way to the Princess Hotel. Drag the left foot to the right foot, twirl, reach up, both hands in the air, clap, smile. She seems so far away, the girl that used to dance in that class. 'Sonny, once so true, I love you-ooo.'

I hurry along. I want to smoke for the first time in ages. I want to smoke and drink another gin and laugh with Claudette. The big sky is dark already, but it isn't far away. There are stars up there, which are the same stars that we have at home but perhaps they taste of different things. Who knows what stars taste of? I giggle. Then I hiccup, it's quite a sore hiccup. Then I giggle again. One thing when I am a bit tipsy is I am good at keeping myself company. When I'm on my own I should just get blotto all the time, then I'd be happy. What funny things fly into my head. Of course you are happy, I tell myself. Don't be such a drama queen. You are not going to ruin Claudette's holiday. You are not going to get tearful and depressed. Repeat, you are not going to ruin Claudette's holiday.

They are still at the bar on the tall stools. Their legs are intermeshed with each other's. I'm shocked at them being so open. Claudette has always been discreet and it's not like this is Lesbos. This is not Lesbos. I zigzag towards them. 'Helloooo,' I say, 'look who's-a here.'

How to get away with suicide

It wasn't going to be easy. For one thing, too much was known about Malcolm. He wasn't one of those sad cases that had no friends. By the time he was forty-five, he'd gathered arguably too many friends. They knew, for instance, that Malcolm was a very good driver and there was no way in the creation that he'd end up with his metal wrapped around a lamppost, or with his bonnet stuck in the birch tree at the end of his old street, or his car up-ended on the central reservation of the M8 to Edinburgh. 'Reserve your judgements on that one,' he could imagine his pals saying, softly, 'cos Malkie wis an excellent driver. All right – one drink-driving offence, but Malkie never knocked down anything. No no no no. Something's fishy; we're talking suicide here.'

The thing was, Malcolm badly wanted to kill himself: he wanted the noise to stop; he wanted the silence that pads across a loch on a wintry, misty morning with its webbed feet. No more demands, Malcolm wanted not to have to tell himself all the ways in which he hadn't really done what he thought he might do with his life. But he didn't want anybody knowing he'd killed himself. Just because he wanted to die didn't mean he'd lost his pride. That might be a contradiction for some people to think about; and some people might think that if you got that desperate you really wouldn't care what people thought. You would actually be beyond it. Well, Malcolm wasn't beyond it. He respected the living. Face it: suicide's a bum deal. He didn't want his mates feeling bad for years, thinking, Right enough, he didn't sound himself. Should have taken him for a pint. Or should have this, should have that. He didn't even want his ex-wife to feel rotten, despite the not insignificant fact that she was the one that dumped him, took his kids and got a big stupid eedyit to prance around and pretend to be their father. Try that out. If somebody's pretending to be you, Malcolm thought, then who are you? Would it be noticed really, in a significant, life-changing way? He doubted it. He had loved his wife once. He was categorically not interested in revenging her for betraying him. Malcolm would actually be the first to acknowledge that he had been a miserable bastard for years. Katie was entitled to her wee portion of happiness. 'Do you mean that, Malkie?' 'Naw; aye. I wanted to be dead, very dead indeed, more dead than a dodo.' Thinking about death was a non-stop conversation in Malcolm's head. He played the parts, as if a jury were involved. For him acquittal was being allowed to quit, to make a rapid exit, to say, Ta ta, I'm away. Will ye no come back again? No, frankly.

People say if you've got running water you are

lucky; if you've got food you are lucky; if you've got drink you are lucky. If you are hanging around Glasgow Cross out of your mind, with the big black dog snapping at your heels, running water is actually not much use to you. Do you know? You find yourself . . . That's it; you find yourself in situations you wouldn't have put yourself in when you were a boy, staggering outside the Old Tolbooth Bar at the top of Saltmarket near the Gallowgate bawling your eyes out like a baby. Why? Who knows why about anything really. We think we know why and we don't know why and we can't cope with not knowing why; that's about all Malcolm could think to say about why.

But by the way, *why* was not what interested him. *When*, now that was the big juicy question. When could he do it and how, there was another massive word. Hoooooowwwwww. Saying how made him feel good. Howwwwwwwwww. He held on to the *wih* sound. Aye. The two big words coming into Malcolm's brain in the freezing December Glasgow cold were when and how. But not why. Why did not actually get a look-in. How. When. When How. He walked up Buchanan Street, turned left into West George Street, crossed West Nile Street, crossed Renfield Street to Hope Street, walked up the top of Hope Street into Sauchiehall Street. It was chucking it down. The kind of rain that's got fucking cold fingers like your daddy's mammy or, Christ, admit it your ex-wife's. She always had cold fingers. She used to say 'cold hands, warm heart', but that turned out to be nonsense because her heart was certainly not warm. Ice is not even near the ball park. Polar fucking frosty fucking frigid freezer fucking frozen peas heart. But let's not go there. Malcolm tries not to think of Katie these days. It just brings him down and he wants to be up, up up up, enough to enjoy thinking about how he can get away with it. Come on, come on, Malkie, he says to himself, for goodness' sake, son, are you going to be able to pull this one off?

Malcolm had always been a pernickety man who enjoyed puzzles and this was the biggest one of his entire life: how to kill himself and make it look like an accident. When the black dog came for him with its frothy mouth in the winter months of his marriage, he was always kept away from just tying a rope to the garage fucking ceiling because of the offspring, because of Lucy and Jojo and the wee man. But now he is not getting to see his bairns. He says the word bairns when he is full of self-pity, because it brings him close to tears. He likes a word that makes him greet. Katie can tell all the lies she wants, but Malcolm was a good daddy to them and she fucking knows it. So there you are. He didn't just turn the box on, sit them down in front of it like zombies and dump burgers and chips, fish and chips, pie and chips and pizza and chips on the three bairns. No. He did things with them and he made soup and he didn't smoke around them. He made excellent broth, by the way. And was always on the lookout for something interesting to do with them, because Malcolm had taught himself most of what he knew and he wanted to teach them too. He took the bairns to the oldest house in Glasgow. He took them to the art galleries. Malcolm's offspring had been to every place in Glasgow that has a painting: Kelvinside Art Galleries, the Modern Art thingimigig with the different-flavoured floors, near where the old Music and Drama building was. If you've lived in Glasgow as long as Malcolm, you always remembered what buildings used to be where. It was disconcerting, like you were living a double life, half in the dark Glasgow past, long before they ever cleaned up the sandstone.

If Malcolm was a building and he could simply clean up his sandstone, things wouldn't be all that bad. Glasgow's changed; it used to be a very dark city and now it's light. Malcolm considered being a tour guide for Glasgow and he went into the tourist board to make that very suggestion and they took his name and put it in a file. He goes to Buchanan Street bus station to get the bus back to the Milton. He is wary of driving at the moment and anyway road tax has run out. Probably the tourist board will ring up when I've called it all off, when I'm totally dead, Malcolm thought, when the game's a bogey. What else with the bairns, then? Burrell, Christ, even the Burrell, which is a bit out of the way, and used up a lot of petrol. The redundancy money was running out fast, but better spent on art than on shite. The bairns liked that American with the dark paintings in the McLellan

Galleries in Sauchiehall Street, the one whose widow left his brushes and stuff to Glasgow because she didn't want the Yanks tae have his intimate brushes, what was his name? The brain's a sieve. Soon, soon there would be no need to remember anything. Can you imagine the relief of that? Malcolm tried to imagine a time when he wouldn't have to be learning new things, when this burden that he placed on himself of trying to be cleverer than he actually was, was lifted and he was free.

Up until fairly recently, Malcolm had been enjoying listening to classical music. He listened to Radio 3, which was a whole education for him by the way, a complete education. This morning he cried his eyes out when they played Strauss, *Transformation*. It's raining now, very dreich. When it rains like that, dark in the afternoon, you feel like you've been taken into the past. If you can transform, if you can change, maybe you don't have to bump yourself off, you know. If you can transform maybe you can live – Whistler, that's the name. Good. That would have bugged him all day and taken the edge off concentrating on his plan: the total but secret destruction of Malcolm Henry Jobson. Transformation. He got to his small house, turned the key in the door. The hardest thing now about living on his own was returning home to an empty house. Putting the key in and braving it through the hall. It was so quiet in his house; the only thing that welcomed him was the dog. He fell into his bed and slept the drink off for a bit.

He thought about transformation and he looked in the bathroom mirror. Another night on the sauce. Can't even remember falling into his bed. His eyes were hanging out of their sockets, like the sockets were dodgy plugs. His face rough like a dog's arse. He is going bald. He is too wiry; he is not a pretty sight. Her going with Him has made him feel like a wee nyaff. Don't ask him how it's done this, but it's made him smaller in height. When he was married he was five foot eight, now he looks about five five at the most. The new man is a handsome big bastard. He can say that because – quite catastrophically for Malcolm – it's the truth. And he doesn't have a tattoo. Malcolm's got a fucking big stupid tattoo down his arm. A map of Scotland with Katie's name across it and a wee snake in the bottom left-hand corner in blue. She turns her nose up at the tattoo now. It's not fair encouraging your bloke to have a tattoo years ago when you loved the shape of his arse and liked a candy floss in the Kelvin Hall to turn around, years later, when you've gone all hoity-toity because you've gone to a night class and met a posh geezer from Newton Mearns, and say that tattoos are naff. It's no right. Malcolm would have had it removed but he loathes pain and there's no point now anyway. Well, maybe there is. He'll have a think. Does he want to go wherever he is going with this tattoo still on him? is question number one. And question number two is: wouldn't having this tattoo removed, painful though it very well might be, be preparation for the inevitable pain of suicide?

What does she do – the one that said she'd love him forever – to think he used to stop her and say, 'I don't believe in the forever bit, baby, let's live just for today' – she goes off and falls in love with the fair-haired dickhead, hair that falls over his face like a pansy, and presumably, she's told him the same bullshit now, how she's going to love him forever. Well. She's said to him, 'Malcolm' – because she's back to calling him his official name that no one calls him – 'Malcolm, we could have done without your jealousy.' Well, he could have done without it too, you know. Then she said, 'This isn't love, this jealousy, this is just pure selfishness pretending to be love.' It's not enough that she's broken his heart, broken his home and ripped him off, taken his kids, set up with another man who is pretending to be their daddy, you know, but he is to be accused of being selfish?

The other reason Malcolm wanted to kill himself without anybody knowing that he'd done himself in is that people who commit suicide have got a poor reputation and are accused after the event of being selfish. How about that, eh? Can you imagine anything worse? You feel that bad you want the suck of a cold gun inside your mouth and the people surrounding the people left behind mutter at your funeral, 'What a terrible thing to do, what a dreadful selfish thing to do.' I mean fucking excuse me, Malcolm thought.

YOU'RE NOT IN YOUR RIGHT MIND. Trees, flowers, butterflies, children, going to China one day maybe, or going to – where else was it that you wanted to go? Doesn't matter. Friends, your mother, money, work, daft memories, dog, house, none of it matters. All that stuff is all very silly. It's only love that matters in the end and when that goes, you don't frankly give a donkey's toss about anything, anything at all. The only beautiful thing left to you is death. Silence, you know. Like shut the fuck up because I'm no listening to this crap any more; Malcolm was pacing his room now, talking to himself out loud. 'I don't have to do this – live.'

One of the nicest things that happened before they all split the house up was Lucy coming in from school to say that she'd got two house points: one for writing beautiful sentences and the other for writing on the line beautifully with a sharp pencil. Malcolm said to her, 'I'm proud of you, Luce,' and then he went upstairs and threw up in the toilet.

Options. They have that for the movies, don't they? Option this, option that. Option One. Get some deadly poison and take it slowly over a period of time. But the thought of constant diarrhoea and gut pains is not very pleasing. Because Malcolm is a terrible coward when it comes to pain, it is actually very difficult trying to find a solution to his problem. Most methods of suicide are painful whether they look like suicide or not. Throttling yourself must be sore and nobody really knows how long it takes once you kick the chair from under your feet. Ditto slashing your wrists and anyway you couldn't make that look like an accident. He thought of just walking out in front of a car on the bypass but then he'd be giving some total stranger a nasty raw deal; he's got that on his conscience, even if he says to himself, 'There was nothing I could do, he just stepped right out in front of me,' he'll be haunted for years and years to come. He could go up on his roof ostensibly to fix his chimney or TV aerial or something and just fall off. But he is not the kind of bloke that ever goes on his roof. Malcolm is not a handyman. He half envies and half despises handymen. DIY fuckers, fussing over this and that, making a mess actually for people when they move into your house and have to inherit spangled wiring.

Not long after Malcolm was made redundant, he discovered that she was at it with Him. That was a double blow. And he's not short of a bob or two either. You should see the stuff he's bought Malcolm's bairns. Computers and Barbies and GameBoys and Disney dressing-up clothes and DVD machines and a big karaoke machine. Apparently Jamie fancies himself as a bit of a Frank Sinatra. One night before Katie was properly with Jamie, she confessed to Malcolm that Jamie said, 'Only two people can phrase in this world, me and Frank Sinatra.' The tears poured down Malcolm's face, he was killing himself so much.

Malcolm is not into material things in any case.

Never needs much to get by. He doesn't think it's good for kids to get this and then get that and then get something else. But when, in the early days (when she was still letting him see them before she took out a court order just because he took a hammer to the new computer like a Luddite), he said anything about materialism, she just raised her eyebrows and said, 'Sour grapes, Malcolm, be happy for us. The kids don't want for anything now and that's lovely for them.' He is supposed to be happy when his kids have transformed before his very eyes into spoilt brats. He is supposed to welcome this? Being in love has made his ex-wife very insensitive. Here's a wee example: 'I'm sorry, Malcolm, but now that I'm with Jamie, I really know what love is. I thought it was love with you, but it wasn't. I can't help my feelings. Every time I see him I go weak at the knees.' When she said that to Malcolm, strange music came into his head, angry octaves that he'd been listening to the day before. A piece by Schubert, if he remembers correctly. The man wasn't well when he wrote it. Poor bastard. Some of that music is no right in the head. It gets right in and starts to play itself to you even when it's not playing. He blinked, that time, and didn't say anything. On the one hand, she was hyper-sensitive to Jamie and everything he wanted and all his feelings. Malcolm couldn't go in when he went to pick up his kids because Jamie found it difficult. He couldn't ring after six because Jamie found it difficult. He couldn't fucking breathe because Jamie found it difficult. *It'll no be long now.* And on the other hand she didn't seem to give a horse's toss about Malcolm's feelings. She was like a woman driven, a woman possessed.

Och, enough. He loved her and she didn't love him not like he loved her and that is the story – end of story – of most people's love. There's always somebody who loves a bit more; somebody who loves a bit less. I'd be surprised if that big bastard doesn't break my wife's heart. I hope he doesn't, Malcolm thought. He was still pacing. He was a bit hungry actually, but he couldn't think of stopping for food. He couldn't exactly rush out for a last fish supper. No. He is not petty. Believe you me, he says to himself, I've not got a petty bone in my body. He hopes Jamie doesn't leave her or break her heart because what would be the point of everything he's gone through just for her to end up with a sore heart like his? It's not as if she'll come back to him now. He entertained that for a while. But no. Too far down the road now. Said too many bad things. She actually said to Malcolm that she preferred men that didn't talk so much. 'I prefer the silent types.' Nee naw nee naw nee naw. She said, 'You don't talk, Malcolm, you rant. On and on and on as only you can go and I'm tired of it, Malcolm, I'm tired of you ranting.' Blaaah di blah di blah. Excuse me? Glasgow is jam-packed with ranting men. Aaaaaaach. A good rant is good for you like a big bowl of porridge. He sometimes feels as if porridge is coming out of his mouth when he is ranting. Splurge. Grey. Lumpy. Thick.

At least he admits his bad points. Give him his due. He is messy. He is prone to a bit of ranting here and there. He has a temper. He is prone to depression. He doesn't get round to doing things as quickly as he should these days. What does the ex-wife admit to? Bugger all. She's got no faults whatsoever by the way, she's perfect. She was perfect, you know. He wishes he'd seen that at the time. He wishes he'd seen that when she lay in bed next to him for fifteen years. She said to him a month or so ago, 'It's been a long time, Malcolm, move on. You're a long time dead. Get yourself a new girlfriend.' But he is not interested, has absolutely not a bit of interest in lumbering himself with a new girl-friend. The only thing he is interested in is in killing himself. That's the one thing he finds exciting. That's the big thrill in his life at the moment. In any case, he's not certain he'd manage that whole business any more. It's all right for women; they can fake it but for a man it's a little bit obvious, you know. He is frightened. He is more frightened of never getting a hard-on ever again than he is of killing himself.

It's three in the morning and Malcolm is just lying here not achieving very much. He lights up a smoke and stares at the ceiling. He is so crap he can't even come up with a decent plan without veering off his subject. He can't seem to stick his mind to anything these days. He used to be able to when he was working. He used to be Mr Malcolm efficient Jobson – 'Ask Malcolm to do something and he will do it.' He may as well get up. He doesn't need to get dressed because he is dressed already. What's the point in taking clothes off when you've only to put them back on again? When the drink wears off, he wakes up. He gets maybe three to four hours' sleep. Maybe you can't even call that sleep. Three hours unconscious and then bang! The eyes open, the thoughts buzz, round and round and round and round in his head. There's nothing new to think. It's just the same stuff that goes round and comes back like a bad digestive system. Like a bat circling the same patch of sky. Malcolm keeps trying to work it out. When exactly she started with him. How she started with him. When how. How, when. He imagines Jamie will be a bit of a Casanova in the bedroom, not that Malcolm was a wham bam thank you ma'am, but still. Aaaaach. Dirty – dirty – dirty.

He goes into his bathroom and takes a leak. It's a long alcoholic leak, bright jaundiced yellow. It goes on for ages and is very noisy. He's a bit jangled. That Schubert is playing again, the Unfinished one they played the other day, playing in his head without the radio on. His kidneys are a bit tender like his balls, his wee disappointed balls. It's cold. This house is cold. There's boxes of his stuff not unpacked yet so that should make things easier for them when they're clearing it all away. He got a letter the other day, can't remember when because the days have got mixed up. It said – wait a minute, here it is in his trouser pocket. Actually, let him have a fag to go with it – 'Dear Malcolm, the kids are missing you and I want everything to be better between us. Would you like to come for your tea? Jamie is fine about you coming for tea and will be here too. For the sake of the kids, let's try a bit harder. Let's forget the past. I promise not to mention the computer again. I don't want to deny our kids their dad. With love, Katie.' He could tell from the wording of that letter that it was not hers, it was his, pretending to be hers. She never, ever wrote *with love*. He didn't even think she'd know that you could do that, write *with love*; she'd know about *warm wishes* and *all the best* if she wanted to be a bit frosty, and *lots of love* if she wanted to be very warm, and plain *love* if she wanted to be non-committal, but not *with love*. She used to write *love* on every single note – even the ones she left about the house asking for him to get more milk. She was a contradiction like that, you know. The things she wrote down were warmer than her in person. That sounds like she's dead, Malcolm thought. Well, in a way, she is, you know, in a way she is dead.

He washes his face with cold water. He brushes his teeth. The toothpaste has run out so he does his best with his brush and tries and makes a mental note. Get some toothpaste, Malkie, because even if you die very soon, you want to die with fresh breath. Ditto being clean. He takes his clothes off and jumps in the shower. He washes his body. He washes his legs and in between his toes and behind his ears and behind his neck like his mother taught him. The soap is wearing thin and slithering out of his hand onto the floor. He can see through it. He gets out of the shower and dries himself with a damp towel. Katie was right – you should hang the fucking towels up or else when you come to use them again they're damp and you're full of regret. He tries to find a pair of clean boxers. This is a bit of a challenge by the way and he can't remember when he last did a big wash. He looks inside his machine and there's a whole wash in there damp as well and smelling the way a wash does when it's not taken out and hung up, like smelly socks or something bad you ate that comes back to you. Christ, Malkie, he says to himself, if you're going to kill yourself, you're going to have to get a bit more organized.

He doesn't like the idea of being dead and Katie coming round here to clear away his things and seeing the state of the place. That would be a dead giveaway as well. It's half-past three in the fucking morning and he's hoovering his place, standing starkers in his bollocks because he can't find clean boxer shorts and he's put some on the radiator to dry. It's freezing and he feels a bit pervy being naked and hoovering until he has a brainwave. He rushes back to his bedroom and hunts through his drawers. He pulls everything out, jumpers, T-shirts, sweatshirts, God he needs to sort all this out, this is out of order, till finally he finds them. He puts on his old swimming trunks, that's better. He taught all his bairns to swim, by the way: breast stroke, crawl, even butterfly. People doing the butterfly

look mental, don't they. What a contortion the butterfly is.

He can't remember when he last got the fucking
hoover out either. It's like the months since they split
have passed in a fug. The fucking thing isn't picking
up properly. Bastard fucking hoover! He takes the
bag out and empties it in the kitchen bin and half of
it goes in the bin and the other half of it falls on the
floor. Grey munchy dust; maybe that's what heaven looks
like. Maybe heaven isn't white at all but more like
clouds of hoover dust. Who knows? He'll not be finding
out because even if he manages to hide his suicide from
all his living relatives, he won't be hiding it from God
supposing there is a God. He must admit you start to
have your wee doubts when you're involved in a big
plan like this. Put it this way, you are more likely to
say you're an agnostic than an out-and-out atheist at
this stage in the game.

He attaches the hoover bag into the hoover again
which takes ages because his hands are trembling.
Stupid things. Trembling like fucking Muhammad
Ali's hands in the end, you know. Big Cassius Clay,
what a man, eh? He remembers years ago before they
had a telly, when he was a boy, standing outside a telly
shop in Argyll Street with about a hundred other people
crammed and jammed against the window watching
the big match between him and Foreman out in the
street.

He turns the hoover on again. The dog runs out of

the room. It's only when the dog does that and he sees the wary look in the dog's eye that he thinks to himself: Christ, the dog. He'd forgotten all about the dog even though he'd been feeding it. He'd not considered the dog's role in his private life, in his topping himself. The dog is a bit of a problem, really. Another thing he is going to have to chew over. That Jamie doesn't like dogs is the only reason he has got the dog. His kids will miss their dog and he doesn't want to kill the dog too. What's she done? Actually she's the only one that's really been his pal during all this autumn through to winter. The amount of times that dog has looked into his eyes; he swears she knows his secret. She gives him this despondent, self-pitying look that is quite something to behold.

No matter. He'll consider that later. Polo would be happier with the kids anyway. Polo misses the kids and the wife. And if he were actually gone, then Jamie would have to be persuaded. Polo has had a hang-dog expression ever since the house was sold and they came to live in this wee place in the Milton. The wife is living in the Briggs. At first they thought that would be easier for them, not that far between them. They might be just a few miles down the road from each other, but Malcolm actually feels like they are living in different universes. He doesn't recognize her, do you know. Maybe it's me, maybe it's all me, he thinks to himself. He first knew that he was depressed when he lost interest in football. He'd been a big Celtic fan all his life since the days of Kenny Dalgleish, the first. Suddenly there he was one day a couple of years ago, big match on the telly and he turned it over. Years of him saying wheeesht to his kids when the football was on only to have no kids and no football now. No telly, actually. When he was working he had a season ticket and went all over the fucking place with the football. He was in Barcelona once and he said to his pals, 'Look at the bloody Spanish, aren't they good-looking?' He wasn't even commenting on the women; it was the men, actually. Good-looking big bastards. He said to his pals, 'We Scottish must be the ugliest bunch of bastards in the world.' And one of his pals said, 'Speak fir yoursell.'

If he went out with the dog, drove over the Campsie Glens into the Fintry Hills and just set off on those rough-looking moors when the temperature is below freezing with a bottle of Bell's, the dog would probably get found by somebody. That was one possibility. Drink the bottle and lie down in the cold in such a way that looks like he's fallen over. And freeze to fucking death. No but he doesn't fancy that much, though. Too chilly. What else. C'mon, Malkie, think. Use the loaf. Use the head. All the usual paths for the blue people are closed to him. He can't take pills. There has to be a way.

It's four thirty now and it's still very dark outside. Very wintry dark. He goes right outside and looks up at the stars. Every constellation you could name or imagine is up there tonight; the stars have a ball when it's freezing cold. He was teaching Jojo about the stars a few months back, well those he knows anyway. The Plough, the Bear, the brightest planet. Jojo got up because Jojo heard them fighting and he took him out for a wee minute to look at the stars and Katie came out and said, 'Are you out of your mind, he'll catch his death.' He goes back inside the house that doesn't feel like his and opens the curtains properly. Quiet out there in the Milton. Hardly any lights on. One or two, probably old insomniacs, mucking about in their kitchens, getting a cup of tea or talking to their cat. Not a huge amount goes on at this hour during the week anyway. He goes to light a cigarette and thinks to himself that he may as well give up smoking. It's one thing he could actually achieve before he dies. He could say to himself, Well at least before you died you gave up smoking. The same goes for drinking when he thinks about it. Today on his last day he is not under any circumstances whatsoever going to drink and he is not going to smoke which rules out the Fintry whisky option. Even supposing it takes him another three weeks to pull it off, a fag will not cross his lips or a wee nip of anything, no Bell's, no Teacher's, no special malts. Absolutely, unequivocally nothing. Not a nippy nothing. In the middle of the night, with his swimming trunks on and the hoovering finished, Malcolm Henry Jobson makes up his mind to straighten himself up before he takes himself out.

Blinds

The Blind man arrived at nine thirty to measure my windows. I've not long moved in and am up very late most nights adjusting to the new house and its different noises. The boiler is quite different to the old house. And there is a strange loud clunk every time the toilet is flushed or the cold tap turned off. Nine thirty felt quite a challenge for me to be up and showered and dressed for the Blind man. I was more than eager to have them measured and made because I am now living in a terraced house and next door can see right into my kitchen. One of the women next door waves the minute she sees me, which I find disconcerting. I lived in a corner house before and never saw anybody from any of the windows. We all want friendly neighbours, of course. But too-friendly neighbours fill us with alarm and dread.

I made the Blind man a pot of fresh coffee. Something about him suggested to me that a cup of instant would offend his senses. I still had lots to be getting on with, boxes here and there that needed emptying, a heart that needed sorting, but I thought to myself, What kind of human being are you if you can't make a fresh pot of coffee for a man who has come to give you privacy? I've taken two weeks off work to settle in. It still feels like somebody else's house. I feel like I am play-acting my life living here.

I measured four heaped spoons from the brown plastic spoon into my brand-new cafetière. I found two new white mugs in the new cupboard. I told the man I had chosen different colours for each of my three kitchen windows. 'Very Chorlton,' he said. 'Very trendy.' Then he said, 'Very *brave*.' This made me feel a little queasy. I had never had the chance to choose everything. I've always lived with extremely assertive people, so I am not quite confident in my tastes. I got the milk out from the fridge even though I guessed he was going to say he liked it black and strong. 'Why should choices about carpet colours and so on worry us so much?' I said. 'I've woken myself up in the night worrying about the colours. When you think of all the problems in the world and all the things there are to worry about, isn't it horrifying to wake yourself up worrying about the colour of your kitchen blinds, or the floor tiles or the colour you have chosen for the hall carpet?'

'These are big choices,' he said. 'Choices are scary. All choices. All decisions. Scary stuff. The amount of people that take ages to make a choice, then we go, we fit the new blinds to their window, whatever kind they like, roller or Roman or Venetian, and they scratch their head and stare and then say in such a terrible disappointed voice, "Oh, they don't look like how I thought they'd look." And I say, "And what did you think they'd look like?" And they look back, blankly, and say, "Oh I just thought, I don't know, I thought that peach would be richer. Or that plum would be plummier." And the voice trails off, you know. Like it has entered some world where the colour they truly wanted does not actually exist. Oh, it's terrible, terrible.'

I nod. I can't quite shake the uneasy feeling. How do I know when they come and put up my three different colours, my brique (which nearly put me off being spelled with a q), my damson and my terracotta, that I won't be like the women he describes? 'It must be lovely to be decisive,' I say wistfully. 'Mustn't it? Don't you envy the people that make decisions and stick to them?' He sips his coffee, considering. 'Yes and no,' he says after some time, 'yes and no.'

I'm not sure whether it is the fact that I am up too early or feeling hungover or even that I am quite lonely in my new life, but the Blind man's 'Yes and no' sounds to me like rocket science. It sounds the real thing. Who needs Freud or Derrida when the man comes and says yes and no like that and sips his coffee pensively? 'I am a self-made man,' he says to me. 'I have been this successful because I've said no and I've said yes and sometimes I've had to admit my mistakes. I still keep my hand in at the measuring so as I keep in touch with people.' He pats my dog. 'Nice dog,' he says. 'I haven't seen that kind before. What kind is it?' 'It's a Tibetan terrier,' I say. 'My mother says there's something wrong with people that don't like animals. Here's my mother for you.' The Blind man steps out to the middle of my kitchen floor and opens his arms. 'Here's my mother.' He is a man of about fifty-five with dark brown hair and a handsome face, very polished shoes. He's wearing a smart designer suit. 'Here's my mother. All religious people are sexual misfits. All people that don't like children are weirdos. All children that aren't allowed to mix with other children are vessels for their parents. Oh yes.' He closes his arms and clasps his hands together tightly as if he is praying. His voice has changed while he does his mother. He's adopted a thick, slightly comical, Irish accent. 'She's quite defin-ite you see about everything. There's not a thing she doesn't have an opinion on. She could do with a bit of yes and no.'

I pour him some more coffee. He still hasn't meas-ured my windows, but what the hell. He's been here in my new kitchen for half an hour. 'I've got very confused about everything. I can't decide whether to have the brique-colour one on that window or that one,' I say pointing to the bottom window and the middle one. I notice the woman next door at the sink. She is wear-ing her glasses and a top I haven't seen her in yet. He says, 'Make sure that the very different colours go next to each other so it looks deliberate. You don't want to look as if you've just run out of colour and gone for the next nearest thing.' 'Oh no! I definitely don't want that!' I say, the alarm rising in my voice. The next-door neighbour waves at her window and smiles. I smile back. I can see her looking at the Blind man wondering who I have got in. I've had so many men in the house recently and they all end up in the kitchen with me having a cup of something: the carpet man, the shelf man, the boiler man, the bathroom man, the kitchen man. The carpet man told me all about his marriage problems and liked my choice of carpet colour in the hall so much that he said I should take up interior designing. I slept so well that night – bliss. 'So,' he says, 'I would go for this one on that window, this one on that one and this one on that one.' He sips the fresh mug of strong black coffee. 'My mother has been driving me insane recently. It's not her fault. She is grieving the love of her life who wasn't my father. The last fifteen years of her life she has had with this man. They went out on lots of lovely drives together. And her big problem is what to do with the car – the lovely little car that took them on all those special day trips, to the Lakes, to the Peak District, to Derwent Water, over the Snake Pass. She doesn't want to sell it and she doesn't want it sitting in the drive. She's shifted all her grief onto that small red car.' 'Give it to me,' I say, half-joking. 'I could do with a car.' 'It's in beautiful nick. It's MOTed up to its eyeballs.' I imagine lovely bright headlamps. 'The upholstery and the engine, everything is perfect. She'd love you to have it. She would like you, my mother. What is it she says about the Scots? You can trust a Scot before you can trust an English person. So that's sorted. I'll bring you the car when we get the papers back. It's a fair exchange, this is very good fresh coffee. My mother always says trust your instincts about people. My mother prefers my brother to me even though he never sees her; I'm the one that does everything for her.' 'The ones that are the most loving are not the ones that are most appreciated,' I say. 'You're not wrong,' he says. I notice his eyes have filled. 'My blind company is the most successful in the whole of the country. I've worked myself up from nothing. The wife thinks I'm too generous. But my mother says generosity never goes wasted.' He looks out my bottom window. The sky is big outside, big and blue and bright. 'Right,' he says. 'I'd better get out the measuring tape. Do you want them inside the frame of the window or outside?' 'Inside,' I say decisively. He clambers up onto the kitchen surface and starts measuring the bottom window.

'Actually, I've not long got the dog back,' I say quickly. I don't know why. I just want to tell him because he has been telling me about his mother and because he is giving me a red car. He looks round from measuring the bottom window, the one that looks out onto the corrugated-iron shed and the graffiti and the waste ground. He makes a note in his little book. 'Did you have a custody fight over the dog, then?' he laughs. 'Yes and no,' I say. 'Did he want to keep the dog, then?' 'Yes,' I say and I hesitate and then I say, 'She.'

He doesn't miss a beat. 'My mother says a dog chooses its master. The master can't really choose the dog. Did the dog follow you more or her more?' he asks. He is on the second window now. 'Me more – definitely,' I say. For some reason I feel very shy in my kitchen and can't wait for the roller blinds to be fitted and pulled down. 'How long will it take for them to be made?' I ask as if it was a life-or-death question. 'Two weeks, not more than two weeks. We are very quick. My mother says, if a person is reliable that's all another person wants really at the end of the day.' 'I think I love your mother,' I say. 'I think I'll love her car.'

'That's what she needs, somebody to look after her car and to love her car. You see the car has become him now. And she looks out at it in the drive and she says she just can't bear to see it.'

'I got the dog. She got the car,' I say.

'Well, a dog is better than a car,' he says.

'I'll tell you a story, right,' he says, looking back at me from the third window. 'Are you sure you are getting these right,' I say. 'What if we've been so busy talking about cars and dogs and broken hearts that we get the blinds all wrong?' 'Not possible,' he says. 'Anyhow who said anything about a broken heart?' 'Your mother's heart sounds pretty broken,' I say. I have my hand across my chest. It is quite tight. It must be to do with getting up so early. 'It is. I've never seen grief like it. Grief like that, it's like an animal. She's not eating. She's not sleeping. She's whimpering. She's sluggish.

71

She's not herself. She's not my mother. The least thing and the tears come. And it's me that gets it. I'm the one that's there.'

'I haven't told my mother yet. I've just told her I moved.' The Blind man stares at me. 'Oh, really?' he says. 'Well my mother always says: do things in your own time. Everybody should live how they choose. We never know what goes on behind the blinds.' He laughs as if it is his first cheap joke of the day and it has made him frivolous. 'Is that a line you say a lot?' I ask him laughing. 'Well, even Blind men have to have some patter.' He makes for the door. 'I'd better be off. Lovely coffee, perfect coffee. You'll have a dog and a car and three new brave blinds. What more could you want?'

I smile at him. 'What does your mother have to say about blinds?' I ask him. 'Oh, she hates blinds – especially the Venetian ones; she's a curtains woman. She's for the curtains if she goes on sobbing at this rate.' We shake hands again.

My neighbour appears at her window again and stares in. 'My mother says never trust a weak hand-shake,' he says and shrugs his shoulders. He must be about fifty-five. On impulse he leans towards me and kisses my cheek. 'I will be back with the car,' he says. I don't believe he will. I don't believe he believes he will either. I wave him goodbye. He opens the door of his black BMW by pressing his key. He takes off, waving. I close my door. It is ten past eleven and what have I done today? I have got my windows measured and showered and made some coffee. Days in the new life can be measured slowly, I say to myself. Now it is time to take the dog for a long walk. I shout, '*Walkies, walkies!*' I've noticed I've started talking to the dog out loud more since I've left her. 'Who's Mummy's good dog?' I say. 'Mmmmm? Who is Mummy's good dog? What is love like?' I say to the dog, 'What is love like?' My neighbour appears at her sink again. I think she must be making soup. Her lover comes behind her and kisses her on the cheek. I get the lead down from its hook. The blinds will arrive in two weeks and then I will be able to shut my eyes.

The silence

The last thing he said to her was on a Sunday morning. It was wet outside and he could smell the rain on the grass from the open window. A car passed by in the street and he heard the whisper of tyres in the rain. He wiped his glasses and stood looking out at their back garden. She said, 'Sit down and eat your breakfast. Why do you have to pace up and down all the time? You make me agitated.' And he sat down still looking out of the window. The garden looked empty, disappointed in itself, like somebody turning up at a party empty-handed. The bushes were bare. He said, 'Why is there no colour in our garden?' She said, 'It's the wrong time of year for colour.' He said, 'Do you think we plant things at the right time of year?'

She gave a little indignant noise. Uh. She prided herself on her garden; he knew that. Only he wasn't one hundred per cent sure she knew her onions. 'I read somewhere you can have colour all year round,' he muttered.

She was reading her newspaper and eating her boiled egg. She was a noisy eater and some of the egg yolk was actually on her chin. She said irritably, 'Hold

77

on, I'm reading this, give me a minute's peace at my breakfast.' He thought to himself, I'll give her a minute's peace. I'll give her all the peace she needs. Quite deliberately then, with no irony as far as he was concerned, he said it. A very plain sentence. No emotion in his voice. 'I'll shut up, then.'

And she looked up at him for a second, sharply, and when she couldn't quite read his expression she looked back down at her paper.

You notice things. You're not sure when you start. It's only when you've noticed — noticed that you know you've noticed. Maybe between the first time when you're starting to think, Is this what I think it is? and the second time when you think, Yes, between those two times, there's a silence. A pause. Like snow sitting on a wall, the way snow does for ages looking fairly contented and thick before it falls off. It was that way with us.

He didn't think about how he'd loved her once or thought he'd loved her because it seemed now as if his life was lived by some other man and that she was some other woman. They didn't even look like themselves when he looked at old photographs. It wasn't that they had aged. It was that love had fallen off their faces. When he thought of love, he thought of it with some distaste now. It was like a small wounded animal that couldn't run, that hid in a corner, quaking and shaking.

I said to him, 'What do you think we should have for our

dinner tonight?' and he said nothing. He didn't say 'Nothing' out loud. I mean there was silence. He's been a sulker since I first married him. When he's sulking he sucks in his cheeks so that his face looks an awful lot slimmer. And his eyebrows wriggle around his forehead like worms. That evening there was his Bach in the background. There was the flapping of his newspaper. There was the high cry of kids playing ball out in our street, strange music as if the kids existed in the past, a long time ago, like echoes of children. I listened. I could hear each noise distinctly. And I didn't know why I was noticing these things so sharply. Later, I said, 'I'm turning in,' and I felt myself slip inside myself, a wife inside a wife, a Russian doll. I rubbed night cream on my cheeks. I left the light on for him. I heard the key shutting the door up, his heavy tread on the stairs. I said, 'You've got all the covers.' Next morning I said, 'Do you want some porridge? Do you think we should get a bench for the garden? What do you think of what's happening in France, in Palestine?'

I kept my voice light. 'Listen to this.' I read him bits from the paper. I said, 'Will you let the gas man in, because I'm going out?' I said, 'Do you want me to get your pension?' Nothing, nothing. Silence.

He found with practice that he could actually blot her voice out and truly not hear it. He'd see her lips move but the sound wasn't there. It was as if she was speaking under water, or in the fog.

We need some more fish food and some toilet roll. What

*do you fancy for your dinner tonight? Do you have a notion
for anything?*

He found himself climbing the stairs of his house
remembering the things he'd said in the past. When
she was made redundant, he said, 'You take the rough
with the smooth.' When she had her operation, he
said, 'You don't look too bad.' When their son was in
trouble, he said, 'I told you I warned you I warned you
I told you.' On their anniversary one year, he turned to
his daughter and said, 'She's a good-looking woman,
your mother.' He sang when her mother died. *The
Lord's my Shepherd, I'll not want . . .*

*I was out in the garden, planting and humming. I saw the
fish were still alive after the winter, one flashed bright orange,
and I wanted to shout him and tell him, but I stopped myself.
I stood and stared at them darting about under the dirty
water of the pond. 'The pond needs cleaning,' I said and he
appeared at my side and started cleaning it.*

He wakes in the deep dead of night. He reaches for his
glass of water and gulps some down, thirsty in the darkness. There was a waterfall once years ago. He remembers
listening to the noise of its hysterical laughter. He
can hear the sound of her breathing, quite long deep
breaths.

His breathing is louder now he is silent. I can't see him

in the dark but I can hear him. *The sound of his sleep, the snores and sighs and small noises, is company.*

He sleeps the sleep of the deep now.

Straight off and away into the dreamy dark. I've never had so much peace in my life.

No one is in his ear. No one is at him.

Saying, I don't think that is how it's done. Saying, Are you sure about this. Saying, I doubt that very much. Nothing. Just sounds. Sounds and more sounds. And silence. Silence and more silence. Thick like snow.

My daughter the fox

We had a night of it, my daughter and I, with the foxes screaming outside. I had to stroke her fur and hold her close all night. She snuggled up, her wet nose against my neck. Every time they howled, she'd startle and raise her ears. I could feel the pulse of her heart beat on my chest, strong and fast. Strange how eerie the foxes sounded to me; I didn't compare my daughter's noises to theirs. Moonlight came in through our bedroom window; the night outside seemed still and slow, except for the cries of the foxes. It must have been at least three in the morning before we both fell into a deep sleep, her paw resting gently on my shoulder. In my dream I dreamt of being a fox myself, of the two of us running through the forest, our red bushy tails flickering through the dark trees, our noses sniffing rain in the autumn air.

In the morning I sat her in her wooden high chair and she watched me busy myself around the kitchen. I gave her a fresh bowl of water and a raw egg. She cracked the shell herself and slurped the yellow yolk in one gulp. I could tell she was still a little drowsy. She was breathing peacefully and slowly, her little red chest rising and falling. Her eyes literally followed me from counter to counter to cupboard, out into the hall to pick up the post from the raffia mat and back again. I poured her a bowl of muesli and put some fresh blueberries in it. She enjoys that. Nobody tells you how flattering it is, how loved you feel, your child following your every move like that. Her beady eyes watched me open my post as if it was the most interesting thing anybody could do. The post was dull as usual, a gas bill and junk. I sighed, went to the kitchen bin and threw everything in but the bill. When I turned back around, there she still was, smiling at me, her fur curling around her mouth. Her eyes lit up, fierce with love. When she looked at me from those deep dark eyes of hers, straight at me and through me, I felt more understood than I have ever felt from any look by anybody.

Nobody says much and nothing prepares you. I've often wondered why women don't warn each other properly about the horrors of childbirth. There is something medieval about the pain, the howling, the push-push-pushing. In the birthing room next door, the November night my daughter was born, I heard a woman scream, 'Kill me! Just kill me!' That was just after my waters had broken. An hour later I heard her growl in a deep animal voice, 'Fucking shoot me!' I tried to imagine the midwife's black face. We were sharing her and she was running back and forth between birthing stations. She held my head and said, 'You're in control of this!' But I felt as if my body was exploding. I felt as if I should descend down into the bowels of the earth and scrape and claw. Nothing prepares you for the power of the contractions, how they rip through your body like a tornado or an earthquake. Then the beautiful, spacey peace between contractions where you float and dream away out at sea.

Many of my friends were mothers. I'd asked some, 'Will it hurt?' and they'd all smiled and said, 'A bit.' A bit! Holy Mary, Mother of God. I was as surprised as the Jamaican midwife when my daughter the fox came out. I should have known, really. Her father was a foxy man, sly and devious, and, I found out later, was already seeing two other women when he got me pregnant, that night under the full moon. On our way up north for that weekend, I saw a dead fox on the hard shoulder. It was lying, curled, and the red of the blood was much darker than the red of the fur. When we made love in the small double bed in Room 2 at the bed-and-breakfast place by Coniston Water, I could still see it, the dead fox at the side of the road. It haunted me all the way through my pregnancy. I knew the minute I was pregnant, almost the second the seed had found its way up. I could smell everything differently. I smelt an orange so strongly I almost vomited.

When the little blue mark came, of course it couldn't tell me I was carrying a fox, just that I was pregnant. And even the scans didn't seem to pick anything up, except they couldn't agree whether or not

I was carrying a girl or a boy. One hospital person seemed sure I was carrying a son. It all falls into place now of course, because that would have been her tail. Once they told me the heart was beating fine and the baby seemed to be progressing, but that there was something they couldn't pick up. She was born on the stroke of midnight, a midnight baby. When she came out, the stern Jamaican midwife, who had been calm and in control all during the contractions, saying, 'Push now, that's it, and again,' let out a blood-curdling scream. I thought my baby was dead. But no, midwives don't scream when babies are stillborn. They are serious, they whisper. They scream when foxes come out a woman's cunt though, that's for sure. My poor daughter was terrified. I could tell straight away. She gave a sharp bark and I pulled her to my breast and let her suckle.

It's something I've learnt about mothers: when we are loved we are not choosy. I knew she was devoted to me from the start. It was strange; so much of her love was loyalty. I knew that the only thing she shared with her father was red hair. Apart from that, she was mine. I swear I could see my own likeness, in her pointed chin, in her high cheeks, in her black eyes. I'd hold her up in front of me; her front paws framing her red face, and say, 'Who is mummy's girl, then?'

I was crying when she was first born. I'd heard that many mothers do that – cry straight from the beginning. Not because she wasn't what I was expecting, I was crying because I felt at peace at last, because I felt loved and even because I felt understood. I didn't get any understanding from the staff at the hospital. They told me I had to leave straight away; the fox was a hazard. It was awful to hear my daughter being spoken of in this way, as if she hadn't just been born, as if she didn't deserve the same consideration as the others. They were all quaking and shaking like it was the most disgusting thing they had ever seen. She wasn't even given one of those little ankle-bracelet name tags I'd been so looking forward to keeping all her life. I whispered her name into her alert ear. 'Anya,' I said. 'I'll call you Anya.' It was the name I'd chosen if I had a girl and seemed to suit her perfectly. She was blind when she was born. I knew she couldn't yet see me, but she recognized my voice; she was comforted by my smell. It was a week before her sight came.

They called an ambulance to take me home at three in the morning. It was a clear, crisp winter's night. The driver put on the sirens and raced through the dark streets screaming. I had to cover my daughter's ears. She has trembled whenever she's heard a siren ever since. When we arrived at my house in the dark, one of the men carried my overnight bag along the path and left it at my wooden front door. 'You'll be all right from here?' he said, peering at my daughter, who was wrapped in her very first baby blanket. 'Fine,' I said, breathing in the fresh night air. I saw him give the driver an odd look, and then they left, driving the ambulance slowly up my street and off. The moon shone still, and the stars sparkled and fizzed in the sky. It wasn't what I'd imagined, arriving home from hospital in the dark, yet still I couldn't contain my excitement, carrying her soft warm shape over my door step and into my home.

When I first placed her gently in the little crib that had been sitting empty for months, I got so much pleasure. Day after endless day, as my big tight round belly got bigger and tighter, I'd stared into that crib hardly able to believe I'd ever have a baby to put in it. And now at last I did, I laid her down and covered her with the baby blanket, then I got into bed myself. I rocked the crib with my foot. I was exhausted, so bone tired, I hardly knew if I really existed or not. Not more than half an hour passed before she started to whine and cry. I brought her into bed with me and she's never been in the crib since. She needs me. Why fight about these things? Life is too short. I know her life will be shorter than mine will. That's the hardest thing about being the mother of a fox. The second hardest thing is not having anyone around who has had the same experience. I would so love to swap notes on the colour of her shit. Sometimes it seems a worrying greenish colour.

I'll never forget the look on my mother's face when she first arrived, with flowers and Baby-Gros and teddy bears. I'd told her on the phone that the birth had been fine, and that my daughter weighed three pounds, which was true. 'Won't she be needing the incubator, being that small?' she'd asked, worried. 'No,' I'd said. 'They think she's fine.' I hadn't said any more, my mother wasn't good on the phone. I opened the front door and she said, 'Where is she, where is she?' her eyes wild with excitement. My daughter is my mother's first grandchild. I said, 'Ssssh, she's sleeping. Just have a wee peek.' I felt convinced that as soon as she saw her it wouldn't matter and she would love her like I did.

How could anybody not see Anya's beauty? She had lovely dark red fur, thick and vivid, alive. She was white under her throat. At the end of her long bushy tail she had a perfect white tail-tip. Her tail was practically a third of the length of her body. On her legs were white stockings. She was shy, slightly nervous of strangers, secretive, and highly intelligent. She moved with such haughty grace and elegance that at times she appeared feline. From the minute I gave birth to my daughter the fox, I could see that no other baby could be more beautiful. I hoped my mother would see her the same way.

We tiptoed into my bedroom where Anya was sleeping in her crib for her daytime nap. My mother was already saying, 'Awwww,' as she approached the crib. She looked in, went white as a sheet, and then gripped my arm. 'What's going on?' she whispered, her voice just about giving out. 'Is this some kind of a joke?'

It was the same look on people's faces when I took

Anya out in her pram. I'd bought a great big Silver Cross pram with a navy hood. I always kept the hood up to keep the sun or the rain out. People could never resist sneaking a look at a baby in a pram. I doubt that many had ever seen daughters like mine before. One old friend, shocked and fumbling for something to say, said, 'She looks so like you.' I glowed with pride. 'Do you think so?' I said, squeaking with pleasure. She did look beautiful, my daughter in her Silver Cross pram, the white of her blanket against the red of her cheeks. I always made her wear a nappy when I took her out in the pram though she loathed nappies.

It hurt me that her father never came to see her, never took the slightest bit of interest in her. When I told him that on the stroke of midnight I'd given birth to a baby fox, he actually denied being her father. He thought I was lying, that I'd done something with our real daughter and got Anya in her place. 'I always thought you were off your fucking rocker. This proves it! You're barking! Barking!' he screamed down the phone. He wouldn't pay a penny towards her keep. I should have had him DNA-tested, but I didn't want to put myself through it. Nobody was as sympathetic to me as I thought they might be. It never occurred to me to dump Anya or disown her or pretend she hadn't come from me.

But when the baby stage passed, everything changed. My daughter didn't like being carried around in the pouch, pushed in the pram or sat in her high chair. She didn't like staying in my one-bedroom ground-floor flat in Tottenham either. She was constantly sitting by the front door waiting for me to open it to take her out to Clissold Park, or Finsbury Park or Downhills Park. But I had to be careful during the day. Once a little child came running up to us with an ice-cream in her hand, and I stroked the little girl's hair. Anya was so jealous she growled at her and actually bared her teeth.

Soon she didn't want me to be close to anyone else. I had to call friends up before they came around to tell them for God's sake not to hug me in front of Anya or she would go for them. She'd gone for my old friend Adam the night he raised his arms to embrace me as he came in our front door. Anya rushed straight along the hall and knocked him right over. She had him on his back with her mouth snarling over his face. Adam was so shaken up I had to pour him a malt. He drank it neat and left, I haven't seen or heard of him since.

Friends would use these incidents to argue with me. 'You can't keep her here forever,' they'd say. 'You shouldn't be in a city for a start.'

'You'll have to release her.'

They couldn't imagine how absurd they sounded to me.

London was full of foxes roaming the streets at night. I was always losing sleep listening to the howls and the screams of my daughter's kind. What mother gives her daughter to the wilds? Aileen offered to drive us both to the north of Scotland and release her into Glen Strathfarrar, where she was convinced Anya would be safe and happy – the red deer and the red fox and the red hills.

But I couldn't bring myself to even think of parting with my daughter. At night, it seemed we slept even closer, her fur keeping me warm. She slept now with her head on the pillow, her paw on my shoulder. She liked to get right under the covers with me. It was strange. Part of her wanted to do everything the same way I did: sleep under covers, eat what I ate, go where I went, run when I ran, walk when I walked; and part of her wanted to do everything her way. Eat from whatever she could snatch in the street or in the woods. She was lazy; she never really put herself out to hunt for food. She scavenged what came her way out of a love of scavenging, I think. It certainly wasn't genuine hunger, she was well fed. I had to stop her going through my neighbour's bin for the remains of their Sunday dinner. Things like that would embarrass me more than anything. I didn't mind her eating a worm from our garden, or a beetle. Once she spotted the tiny movement of a wild rabbit's ear twitching in our garden. That was enough for Anya. She chased the rabbit, killed it, brought it back and buried it, saving it for a hungry day. It thrilled me when she was a fox like other foxes, when I could see her origins so clearly. Anya had more in common with a coyote or a grey wolf or a wild dog than she had with me. The day she buried the rabbit was one of the proudest moments in my life.

But I had never had company like her my whole life long. With Anya, I felt like there were two lives now: the one before I had her and the one after, and they seemed barely to connect. I didn't feel like the same person even. I was forty when I had Anya, so I'd already lived a lot of my life. All sorts of things that had mattered before I had her didn't matter any more. I wasn't so interested in my hair, my weight, clothes. Going out to parties, plays, restaurants, pubs didn't bother me. I didn't feel like I was missing anything. Nor did I feel ambitious any more. It all seemed stupid wanting to be better than the others in the same ring, shallow, pointless. I called in at work and extended my maternity leave for an extra three months. The thought of the office bored me rigid. It was Anya who held all of my interest.

At home, alone, I'd play my favourite pieces of music to her and dance round the room. I'd play her Mozart's piano concertos, I'd play her Chopin, I'd play Ella Fitzgerald and Louis Armstrong. Joni Mitchell was Anya's favourite. I'd hold her close and dance, 'Do you want to dance with me, baby, well come on.' Anya's eyes would light up and she'd lick my face. 'All I really, really want our love to do is to bring out the best in me and in you too.' I sang along. I had a high voice and Anya loved it when I sang, especially folk songs.

Sometimes I'd sing her to sleep. Other times I'd read her stories. I'd been collecting stories about foxes. My best friend, Aileen, had bought Anya *Brer Rabbit*. No fox ever came off too well in the tales or stories. 'Oh, your kind are a deceptive and devious lot,' I'd say, stroking her puffed-out chest and reading her another Brer Rabbit tale. She loved her chest being stroked. She'd roll on her back and put both sets of paws in the air.

But then I finally did have to go back to work. I left Anya alone in the house while I sat at my computer answering emails, sipping coffee. When I came home the first time, the wooden legs of the kitchen chairs were chewed right through; the paint on the kitchen door was striped with claw marks. I had to empty the room of everything that could be damaged, carrying the chairs through to the living room, moving the wooden table, putting my chewed cookery books in the hall. I put newspapers on the floor. I left Anya an old shoe to chew. I knew that no nursery would take her, no childminder. I couldn't bring myself to find a dog-walker: Anya was not a dog! It seemed so unfair. I was left to cope with all the problems completely on my own. I had to use my own resources, my own imagination. I left her an old jumper of mine for the comfort of my smell while I was out working, knowing that it would be chewed and shredded by the time I came home. When I tried to tell my colleagues about Anya's antics, they would clam up and look uncomfortable, exchanging awkward looks with each other when they thought I wasn't looking. It made me angry, lonely.

Sometimes it felt as if there was only Anya and me in the world, nobody else mattered really. On Sundays, I'd take her out to Epping Forest and she'd make me run wild with her, running through the lime trees and hornbeams, through beech trees and old oaks, chasing rabbits. The wind flew through my hair and I felt ecstatically happy. I had to curb the impulse to rip off my clothes and run with Anya naked through the woods. My sense of smell grew stronger over those Sundays. I'd stand and sniff where Anya was sniffing, pointing my head in the same direction. I grew to know when a rabbit was near. I never felt closer to her than out in the forest running. But of course, fit as I was, fast as I was, I could never be as fast as Anya. She'd stop and look round for me and come running back.

I don't think anybody has ever taught me more about myself than Anya. Once, when she growled at the postman, I smacked her wet nose. I felt awful. But five minutes later she jumped right onto my lap and licked my face all over, desperate to be friends again. There's nothing like forgiveness, it makes you want to weep. I stroked her long, lustrous fur and nuzzled my head against hers and we looked straight into each other's eyes, knowingly, for the longest time. I knew I wasn't able to forgive like Anya could. I just couldn't. I couldn't move on to the next moment like that. I had to go raking over the past. I couldn't forgive Anya's father for denying her, for making promises and breaking them like bones.

One morning I woke up and looked out of the window. It was snowing; soft dreamy flakes of snow whirled and spiralled down to the ground. Already the earth was covered white, and the winter rose bushes had snow clinging to the stems. Everything was covered. I got up and went to get the milk. Paw footprints led up to our door. The foxes had been here again in the night. They were driving me mad. I sensed they wanted to claim Anya.

I fetched my daughter her breakfast, some fruit and some chicken. I could tell she wasn't herself. Her eyes looked dull and her ears weren't alert. She gave me a sad look that seemed to last an age. I wasn't sure what she was trying to tell me. She walked with her elegant beauty to the door and hit it twice with her paw. Then she looked at me again, the saddest look you ever saw. Perhaps she'd had enough. Perhaps she wanted to run off with the dog fox that so often hung and howled around our house.

I couldn't actually imagine my life without her now, that was the problem. They never tell you about that either. How the hardest thing a mother has to do is give her child up, let them go, watch them run.

Much later that night when we were both in bed, we heard them again; one of the most common sounds in London now, the conversations of the urban fox.

Anya got up and stood at my bedroom window. She howled back. Soon four of them were out in the back garden, their bright red fur even more dramatic against the snow. I held my breath in when I looked at them. They looked strange and mysterious, different from Anya. They were stock-still, lit up by the moonlight. I stared at them for a long time and they stared back. I walked slowly through to the kitchen in my bare feet. I stood looking at the back door for some minutes. I pulled the top bolt and then the bottom one. I opened the door and I let her out into the night.

What ever

QUAIL

The people in the farmhouse on the top of the hill in Ballantrae have invited Ina McEwan and her family for dinner. They walk from the Hut, a wooden holiday hut lent to them by good comrades, the Haldanes. It is one of those huts with the old gas lights, tiny nets fluttering over the light. Tell Ina what it is about those small lights that makes her feel safe and loved.

The family at the top of the hill are not short of a bob or two. Well, farmers are not poor though they are always complaining. The McEwans' invitation is thanks to young Megan, who makes up for a whole family's strange ways, chattering and giggling enough to hide her mother's odd stops and starts, her father's sullen shyness, her brother's stuttering stammer. At the age of ten, Megan McEwan makes friends with whole families to try and get away from her own, as if asking for help. Megan's father prefers smoking to talking. Her mother does talk sometimes but doesn't listen so her conversation is mad-sounding, because she always speaks as if already in the middle of something.

There are never any beginnings. There are never any endings.

The McEwans put on their holiday best, and as a family walk up the hill, turning one bend and then another and then another. Dogs bark at them from the cobbled farmyards. They can see the sea in the distance and the huge rock of Ailsa Craig, like a relative of theirs who hasn't spoken to them for years, in the huff in the distance. The air smells of hay and cow dung and clover, and this slow walk up the hill is the closest the McEwans ever get to happiness. Near the top of the hill, Megan excitedly says, 'Look, Mum, look,' and there in front of them are a whole family of quails, dumpy, short-tailed, walking across the road, heading for the farmland fields with the cereals and the clover. Ina stares at them, astonished. Quite the thing, the quails. Purposeful and loyal-looking, something about them. Dignified even, yes, dignified is not too strong a word for the quails. Tell Ina why she has never forgotten them or the way her daughter charmed the farmer on the hill that night and covered up every awkwardness with a lovely, beautiful smile, why Ina remembers putting a napkin on her lap and looking round at the chaotic farmhouse kitchen, sipping at a sherry the colour of the hay outside.

When dinner was over, Megan went off to play in the girl's room, was her name Martha? And Ina felt suddenly unmoored like a little fishing boat she'd noticed earlier that day, bobbing out to sea. Megan was in her element – new friend, new toys, new bedroom. Ina still didn't know where she came from, this daughter of hers, or why, when she left a room, she felt uneasy, uncertain of herself. She could feel her mouth opening and closing. She could feel the wail inside herself like a huge wave swelling, about to hit the rocks.

LITTLE TERN

Along the shingle beach, with the sky vulnerable-looking, slightly flushed and pale, Ina walked and walked and walked for miles. Not a soul with her. Not her son, not her daughter, not her man. Along the shingle beach with no company except the sea in all its forgotten rages, battering at the rocks. Ina's face wet with the salt of her tears. She walked on and on as though if she walked far enough she might walk this thing out of her. As if by walking long enough, hard enough, she might forget.

Just ahead of her, a little tern landed on the shingle beach, crying, 'Kirri Kirri.'

If Ina hadn't been so on the ball, so quick to notice things, then it would have been a different story.

The little tern's beak is bright yellow. What is it that gets her most, she wonders, walking, walking, by the sea – a constant, treacherous liar. It is not the thought of the physical thing. It's not even about

Stewart. It's about herself. Now she is all questions, circling in her head like birds. Not questions she wants to ask of him; questions she has to ask of herself. Am I loveable enough? Have I been a good mother? Am I too strict? Do I know how to let my hair down? Little tern. The bird flies off and Ina watches it dive into the sea to hunt for food.

It is possible for Ina to forgive. It is not possible for her to forget. And for years and years after it happened, Ina could still picture herself on the shingle beach, close, quite uncannily close, to that little tern. These days the little tern is a rare bird, having to be preserved, protected from kestrels. It was the place she returned to in her head, the bright-yellow beak on the white beach, the sky bruised and darkening as she walked to a plum colour. How low the dark, how it gathered around the rocks. That night all those years ago, Ina remembers hanging her coat up on the hook, and Stewart looking at her, but not asking where she had been all those hours. Stewart putting the kettle on and making her a hot cup of tea and handing it to her in silence. That night, Ina remembers, she lay in bed as still as anything, listening out for herself. Ina talked to herself, going over things. One slip, she said to herself, lying there with her nightdress buttoned up to her neck. One slip. You cannot penalize a man for one slip. Then she lay wondering about the word slip. When you slip, you fall, but maybe it is not such a sore fall because you have slipped.

Stewart came to bed eventually and placed his hand on her waist and kept it there all night. Earlier, when he brought the mug of steaming hot tea, he had had a look on his face of a man disappointed in himself, so disappointed that he could hardly look up to hand her the tea. But that didn't stop Ina from thinking what he had had with Her was probably better, maybe he'd found something with Her that he had never found with Ina. It didn't stop Ina from thinking that maybe he never loved her at all, not like she loved him, goodness, Ina could love even Stewart's smouldering silences.

And would you believe it, but thirty years later, and still together, Ina found herself asking that question whenever she was a little low. It was the site she returned to, what ever. The little tern swooping down for food, the light draining from the sky. Ina determinedly walking the coastline, her feet on the sore shingle beach. How bright that yellow bill on the bird's mouth, though. No matter how long the love, how deep, Ina still wanted Stewart to say something to her that sounded as nice as the words little tern, as protective, loving. Because the worst of it all was that she had heard a word he had used for Her, a word that still hurt like a sharp flat stone. He had never used that word for Ina. Whenever she was low, Ina said, 'Little tern,' to herself, quietly. Just the words, little tern. Then she saw again the warm glow of late light on the shingle beach.

ROBIN

When someone dies, everyone gets shifty. If you open your mooth to say something small aboot something small, everyone is affie keen to shut you up. I ken it's because they dinny want you going and upsetting yoursell. But dinny they realize talking's no whit upsets you? It's the fact that the deid don't talk that upsets you.

Yesterday I said, Stewart liked a banana on his toast, and that wis me away. You canny tell how it's going to hit you. It comes thundering doon the motorway at a terrific speed in wan o' they long-haul lorries. I says to Janet who was telling me not tae upset masell, I says, Janet it's no something I'm doing tae masell. And Janet says, But you're no helping yoursell. And I says, How am I supposed to help masell? Stewart's deid. Janet says, Don't dwell on it. Try and think of a nice wee warm scone with homemade rhubarb-and-ginger jam. You can get through anything wey the help o' a scone. I just looked at her. Janet is nigh near eighteen stone. She's got wan o' they sweet fat faces – you can see how pretty she wance was. I says, Janet, a scone is not going to solve everything. We've cholesterol to think aboot, and I says, And another thing, hardly anybody bakes a decent scone any more, and I says, Me eating a scone doesn't alter the fact that I've a wardrobe full of claes I canny throw oot, and I says, It comes and gets you in the night. You are that alone your ain body feels different and you try and snuggle into the bed in a position tae comfort yoursell. It might be foetal. And Janet says, Ina, have you gone a bit religious. Janet is wan o' they yins that says things and you dinny understand how her mind has got tae something. I says, How do you mean? Janet says, Would you try and contact him? I says, You mean wey a oudji board? Janet just nods, serious. She pours us both a sherry, as if a wee drink might encourage me to dae something I'd never dae. I sips at it. I like a sherry noo and again. I says, Janet, first it is a scone and noo it's a séance! Have you no ony better advice to give me? Well, Janet says — she's no one to ever be stumped for an answer — another fella? I'm eighty-five, I says. What wuid I be wanting wey another fella? What wuid I do with him? You'd spread a banana on his toast, Janet says and laughs. You know Janet, she's got that loud and daft a laugh. I says I'm no interested in spreading a banana on another man's toast. Well, Janet says, I give up. Anyway, see when she left, I was that exhausted. I slept the hale night weyoot dreaming thon busy dreams that leave you shattered in the morning. That morning I wis making my pot of tea and I looked oot oor back window and it was snowing, and there wis oor wee robin redbreast that visits us every winter and I went tae say, Stewart, the wee robin redbreast is back, and that wis me away again, efter a guid night's sleep tae. Does anybody ken how lang ye go on fir like this because I dinny. I dinny ken. I dabbed at my een and thought, Wait a minute, is that bird no awfie early this year?

I watched it flit aboot the garden and I says to mysell, Stewart is doing OK. And I says to mysell, Right, Ina McEwan, you are going to tackle those claes the day. When I wis finished, I was greeting, but I sat doon at the kitchen and I didnie huv a scone but I had a ginger snap tae my cup o tea and I dooked it in.

GULL

Ina McEwan took pride in the fact that she could still collect her pension. She got up on pension day, got dressed in her slow, measured way, rolling her tights across her bumpy legs. She fitted her skirt to the side of herself. Put her blouse on, her arms through her cardigan and out at the other end. She put her scarf round the folds of her neck which made her think of her sisters in New Zealand, the ones she had survived. She smeared a bit of rose lipstick on her chapped lips and dabbed a bit of powder on her translucent cheeks. She put her pension book in her handbag and got her keys from the key hook. The buttons on her coat were tough as meat. She double-locked her door, shaking it to make sure.

Ina was walking down her street quite the thing, thinking to herself that the older you get, the more you don't take a single thing for granted when the gull swooped down and savagely attacked her head. She stumbled to a neighbour's house, bleeding, trying to think, trying to think, you never know the minute Ina McEwan, trying to think if her sisters had still been alive in New Zealand they would have sent her a special card for this.

Not the Queen

Maggie Lockhart spent her life trying to work out what she'd done to deserve it. There are reasons for things. Things don't just happen, no, they don't. Sometimes the reasons are a long time coming, but when they finally do, they are clearly printed like her pension slip. Most things Maggie worked out to her own satisfaction, though getting people to see the thinking behind the reasoning was hard because nobody took her seriously. Maggie didn't have the temperament for teasing; never had been good at being teased, even as a child, before the nose and the mouth and the cheeks set, but even the most sweet-natured woman would have balked at what Maggie had to put up with. No way in the creation of Christ was it easy going about the place as a kind of a live joke with the Face on it. Nobody could see her face without thinking of the other one's: not the man or the woman in the street, not the total stranger at the bus stop, not even her own family. And even she had the odd feeling when she glanced in the mirror that she wasn't seeing herself, but the bloody Queen. No, no seriously. All right, not dressed in those uptight suits with the buttons, in all sorts of colours from navy to pink to emerald-green, with the scarves, and the bloody brooches and the silly hats, but the Queen just the same. Even with a fag dangling out her mouth and no make-up on, Maggie Lockhart had the bad luck of looking the exact spit of HM Queen Elizabeth the Second.

There had to be some reason that she'd been given the Face. From her teens, Maggie had grown old with the Queen. The Queen was ages with Maggie; Maggie was ages with the Queen. Now they were both in their seventies and it still wasn't making any sense. Oh, she had had her fill of it! Not an overly religious woman, Maggie had some vague notion of a grand plan. Life had to have some sort of purpose or what was the point of it all.

Twenty years ago, Maggie's car broke down on the M8 Glasgow to Edinburgh. When the AA man arrived, he gaped at her, 'Christ, you gave me a fright there, hen.' He lifted her bonnet and peered into her engine. 'Has anybody ever told you, you're the double of—'

'The Queen,' Maggie said, cutting him dead. 'Aye!' he said. 'I'm no kidding but it's a wee bit freaky so it is. Go and look away, will you, while I fix your motor cause you're putting me aff. Jesus, whit a predicament fir ye. An' I suppose this is jist gonna go oan and oan. Whit a burden fir ye, hen.'

It seemed to Maggie that the AA man was the very first person to ever truly understand. She stood nodding on the hard shoulder, as the rain swept across the three

lanes of the motorway, making the road glisten and
sparkle like a ballroom floor. A wee tear came to her
eye and rolled down her cheek. She wiped it away
quickly. She dabbed the end of her round nose. In
Maggie's head, her car had broken down for two
reasons. The first was to stop her having a fatal accident. The second was to hear the AA man say, 'What
a burden for ye, hen.' Twenty years later, Maggie still
hadn't got any further than that. A dour friend would
say pragmatically, 'Well, that was the face you were
born wey,' which was all very well but she wasn't the
one who had to go and get born wey the Monarch's
mug. Maggie couldn't joke about her face; it was no
laughing matter. It had ruined her life. People thinking
one thing about her and then the other. She suspected
some people chose her as their friend just because she
looked like their stamps. Folk doing the big double
take, folk on the make till they realized they'd got the
wrong woman. Fancy your own face being a con; fancy
feeling that you were going about the place trying to
trip folk up. People following her around sniggering
and whispering. There were even jokes about her. Some
people would come and stand outside her small two-up
two-down in Drumchapel. 'Have you heard about the
Glasgow woman that's the spit of the Queen?'

Maggie was as bad as everybody else was. She looked
at her own face and couldn't see the individual. Imagine
that. The thoughts in her head didn't match her face;
how many people had to go around thinking that their

inside thoughts didn't tally with their face? Of course it was all right for Her Majesty. It was plain sailing for Elizabeth. She was the Queen. She could look in the mirror and believe it. Come to think of it, she looked like she did look in the mirror daily and say to herself, 'I am the Queen of England.' But what could Maggie say to herself when her reflection appeared before her? Not a lot. Ever since the AA man's pronouncement, though, she did have something to say. She'd apply a bit of blusher, which made her look even more like her, and she'd say to herself, 'What a burden.' And on really rainy days she'd think, Why me? Are faces accidents? Do they mean anything, faces? Maggie would think to herself when she was a bit squiffy and had had one too many glasses of sparkly spumante.

It seemed to Maggie walking down Sauchiehall Street in town that her face weighed more than other people's faces, heavy on her shoulders. Going out shopping, people often just came right out with it, like the woman at the checkout in BHS who said, 'Oh my God! You're the spitting image. You gave me the fright of my life there!' Maggie was shy and didn't like talking to strangers particularly, never had not even as a child, but the Face made every stranger feel they could pass comment, just like that. She didn't need to have a dog or a baby for complete and total strangers to talk to her; she just needed to look like the notes in her purse. It was rude. Everybody was so rude, so out of order. Cheeky wee madam, Maggie thought to herself when a teenager insisted she was the Queen's twin hiding out in Glasgow. One of Maggie's small satisfactions was talking inside her head to herself throughout the length of a day. What a big stupid glaikit bugger, she'd think as some hefty big guy gave her the eye. Sometimes she wondered if the Queen ever did that, so similar were their faces. What thoughts did she really think about people when she was going about shaking hands and smiling and saying sugary yucky things?

She walked through the shop – same as usual, several ignoramuses performed the open mouth. The Big Stare. She did her best to ignore them. Everybody knew the Queen. Everybody knew what the Queen looked like. Nobody would ever say to the Queen, 'You are the double of Maggie Lockhart' – though Maggie had a great dream the other night when exactly that happened. No, Maggie was the double of the Queen. It didn't work the other way around. The Queen was not the double of Maggie Lockhart. Maybe that was what rattled her. How could you be nobody to yourself?

There are reasons for near enough everything. When the holiday to Tunisia fell through because the bucket shop went bust, Maggie knew that it was probably a good thing; some terrible experience had waited for her there, where she would have got mobbed, literally mobbed.

One year, as she'd stepped off the plane to Cyprus, a whole flock of people had gathered around her. And Maggie had had to wave her hands, 'No, no, no, no!

I'm not who you think I am,' until her Charlie made the crowd vanish. Oh, but Charlie loved it, the swine. The big limping swine loved to see her awkward and embarrassed and to take her arm and rush off as if the pair of them were famous. There was something cloying about Charlie's attentiveness that drove her up the wall from time to time. She came close when he came back from London with a mug with the Queen's face on it. 'No many people can drink their tea and look at their wife,' Charlie had said, raising the mug. Maggie yanked it off him and put it in the box for the jumble.

On the other hand, there were times when it had its advantages. Charlie was always the one to look after her, particularly now they were getting on, the one who did the hoovering, the gardening in their small bit of back garden, changed the bed, because he thought putting a duvet into a duvet cover was too much exertion for her. It was Charlie who always made the cups of tea, who'd bring a steaming mug to her in the living room. 'Yir tea, Maam.' When they walked out, Charlie walked a couple of steps behind her, always on the lookout for any chancers. Once Charlie said to her, 'Dae ye no think we could dae wey a bodyguard fir you?' Charlie was always dreaming up schemes like this. Of course they never had the money, even supposing Maggie Lockhart wanted a bloody bodyguard.

It was a relief now that she no longer worked as a wages clerk after all the comments she'd had to suffer year in year out. People saying, 'It's all right for some,' when she handed over the wages on a Friday. Wee Glasgow blokes all full of themselves as if they were the first ones on the planet to crack a joke. Yug. 'No wee smile? That's like her too. Have you noticed, she hardly ever smiles?' If Maggie had not felt so furious at the Face, she would have by now started feeling a strange sympathy for the Queen. 'Right soor puss. Doesnie even manage a real smile on Christmas Day, fir her own speech.' That was wee Edna. Wee Edna seemed to delight in discussing the Queen's personality with Maggie. 'Do you think she actually feels anything for her children?' wee Edna would say. Or, 'I think she's a bit obsessed with those corgis.' It didn't matter what Maggie said, or what look she gave, wee Edna would read everything about the Queen and come into work announcing confidently, 'The Queen is blazing with Diana, absolutely blazing.' As if Maggie should care, as if any of it mattered to her. 'It bores me to tears, Edna. I'm not the least bit interested.'

And years before, it had seemed that no man would be brave enough to marry Maggie. Then Charlie did. And in bed that first night, to Maggie's absolute horror, he whispered, 'Who's my very own wee Queen, then, eh?' She leapt out of bed and made him swear never, ever to say anything like that again or it would put her off. But it was clear to her looking into Charlie's small eyes that it was the very thing that turned him on. No many men got to see the Queen naked so they didn't no they didn't.

They were always the same age, Margaret Dorothy Lockhart and the Queen of England. There was never any chance of the Queen suddenly getting older and leaving Maggie to get younger or anything like that. So it was a lifelong thing, and after a while Maggie stared at photographs of the Queen in many magazines and would make comparisons. She couldn't help herself, especially when they were both getting on. Not many people had a double to compare themselves to unless they were identical twins and Maggie and the Queen looked the same, so much the same that Charlie would say, 'I'm telling you! Put the pair of you side by side and pit her in your claes and you in hers and not a single bloody person in the whole of England wid be able to tell the difference!' Charlie could get quite het up, as if he was sitting on a goldmine and didn't know how to get at the gold. The Queen had bad posture; Maggie's was better. The Queen had good skin, better than Maggie's skin. (Mind you, think of all the expensive moisturizers.) If you could look into the Queen's eyes for a long time, you'd find that she was shy just like Maggie. The Queen's health was better than Maggie's was too. Maggie had bad asthma and would wheeze when agitated or nervous. Maggie also had irritable bowel syndrome and spent a good portion of her day these days on the toilet cursing and muttering to herself, which was her privilege. She allowed herself that, Jesus and fair enough too. When it came right down to it, Maggie didn't know much personal about the Queen. She knew her favourite dog and horse and castle because wee Edna was always reeling out the facts, but she didn't know anything personal. She didn't know if she liked her nose, or her eyes or her cheeks, if she thought she was attractive or handsome or plain. If she looked in the mirror and felt pleased enough or if she never troubled to think about it, if she just didn't have to think about how she looked at all because she was the Queen whereas Maggie had to think about it because she was not the Queen.

Maggie was a shy and rather diffident Glasgow woman, more like an Edinburgh woman, wee Edna was always saying. Never one to put herself first or forward, Maggie would have been perfectly happy going through life taking a back seat. But the Face made her take a front seat. There she was – stared at from the minute she got up to when she went to bed. When Maggie went to get her hair done, it was always the same. She came out with the bloody Queen's hair even if she'd asked for a frizzy perm. They cut it even when she said, 'I'm growing it.' Year in year out, hairdresser after hairdresser couldn't resist giving her that daft coif, those silly smarmy marmy waves. She could have opened many a library or hospital or theatre, she could have cut many a ribbon. She could have gone about Scotland nodding seriously and saying a few judicious words before pushing people away with her strong handshake.

Once wee Edna and Maggie went to the Bingo and

Edna enjoyed all the people staring at Maggie as if
Edna had taken part in creating her, as if she was a
circus act or some bloody freak show. Edna didn't
even concentrate on her numbers properly for looking
at people looking at Maggie. When Maggie shouted,
'House!' somebody shouted, 'You're rich enough
already,' and her row roared with laughter. Maggie
couldn't be persuaded to go again. 'I'm just not putting
myself through it,' she told Edna to Edna's great
disappointment. Being out with Maggie caused quite a
sensation, quite a commotion.

The day came for Maggie to do something. It finally
dawned on her that there was no good reason for her
having the Queen's face in the way that there were
good reasons for other things in her life. She'd been
patient for ages to wait and to see what the purpose
and the point of it all was. Always a bit philosophical
was Maggie, always one to say reassuringly, if Charlie
didn't get a job promotion, 'What's for you won't go
by you.' Always one to believe that there must be
some intention behind the smallest of things. No such
thing for Maggie as coincidence or accident, things
were meant to happen for some reason. So she'd put
up with her face for years looking in the mirror and
seeing herself and simultaneously the Queen. Well not
for much longer. Maggie was no mug and it was time
she asserted herself. She had been saving on the QT for
some time and had a total of three and a half thousand
pounds. It was a toss-up between really treating her

and Charlie to a cruise or doing what she was going to
do. But the cruise would have been nightmarish, port
after port of people squealing. So that was that then –
decided for her, in a way.

Maggie got up at seven. Her bag was already packed
from the night before. As far as Charlie knew, she was
going to stay with her sister for a couple of weeks. That
would give her the time to get over the bruises and let
things settle. She was having the operation in London
to be as far away as possible from home. On the train
down, Scotland changed into England but she couldn't
see the difference properly.

She'd already been down to London a few months
before to see this particular man that she was putting
her faith in. She'd already told him what she wanted:
a longer nose, higher cheeks, a different chin, and he'd
told her that all that would involve an enormous
amount of work and wouldn't be good for her face at
her age. So they had settled on just changing the nose.
The nose wouldn't cost too much and would change the
look of the whole face.

Of course you get the wind up when you make a
big decision like that, and in the taxi up to the West
End, Maggie was having second thoughts. Had she
not just been a bit touchy all her life? Couldn't somebody who liked a good laugh have enjoyed herself
with the Queen's face? Had Maggie used her face as
a scapegoat to cover her own inadequacies? Would her
life really have been different without the Queen's face?

How? Because it was not as if she had the Queen's money or palaces or anything else, it was not as if she had benefited in any way, but then had she really suffered? Charlie loved her for being herself and looking like the Queen but all husbands had funny ideas about their wives, didn't they? Some husbands liked to see their wives as wee whores as well as wives, so at least her Charlie wasn't that bad, and he'd never been violent and he'd never, ever been aggressive and he'd treated her like his Queen. Christ, wouldn't most not-well-off women give their eye teeth for her Charlie? What would Charlie say if she came back with a different nose? Charlie would be gobsmacked. He would hit the roof. He would say, 'In the name of Christ, Maggie, could you no have consulted me? Whit were ye thinking of, wuman?' And then he would probably cry. Oh God, yes Charlie had only cried twice in his life, when his father died and when Scotland lost in '74, and both times had filled Maggie with a mixture of pity and revulsion, because Charlie hadn't just dabbed at his eyes like she did. Charlie had gone for the whole waterworks, heaving and making a lot of noise and saying, 'Oh Christ! Oh Christ!' bawling his eyes out like a man who hadn't had a chance to cry since he was a boy. It was the thought of Charlie crying that changed her mind. To hell with it. Have the Queen's face and put up with it. Maggie looked out of the black-cab window as it passed Piccadilly Circus only to see some people excitedly looking in. She gave them the smallest of waves.

Pruning

I knew she was having an affair because she told me herself. She said she wanted to respect our fifteen-year-old relationship and not lie to me. I respected her for that. She said that I ought to be grown-up about it and that she wanted to preserve our family, keep our kids together and keep our house. She said I could pick somebody too if I liked because she wasn't bothered any more. She said our life was a whole civilization and she didn't see the point of it all crumbling. She said this woman was the love of her life. I listened in that still way that you listen in the night to a strange sound in your house. I listened without being able to move at all.

We had four children between us and they had grown up together as a family. I didn't want them to suffer either. So I tried. I continued doing the Saturday supermarket shop. I continued to do all of the cooking. Our children's favourite was spaghetti Bolognese made with vegetarian mince. They liked an apple upside-down pudding with fresh egg custard for desert. I ate with them. I never had any of the pudding. She didn't eat with us any more. She said she wasn't hungry and she found the constant sitting down at meals oppressive. She preferred to have some cheese and salami in front of the television with a glass of wine. 'Each to their own,' she said. 'Cheers.'

It was tense between us and I found the radiance on her face when she would come home late after a night out with her lover hard to take. Sometimes she didn't come home at all. I never knew when they would be seeing each other. The dates would happen all of a sudden. All of a sudden she was rushing up the stairs and changing her clothes and putting on some lipstick. I suppose she would never know herself. She would just say, 'I'm going out.'

And if I'd say, 'Where?' she'd just say, 'Out.' And then I'd hear the door slam and the car start up in the drive. I didn't have much to do in the evenings any more because we always spent them together. Even if I had wanted to go out, I would have had to arrange a babysitter. I looked at my own face in the mirror and wondered about it, if it had changed in any drastic way, if it had aged. My eyes looked dark these days and I could do with losing a little weight. I touched up my lips with lipstick more frequently than ever. It became kind of obsessive. I was constantly whipping out my tiny mirror and my jazzy brown lipstick. My black skin looked dusty; I looked like I needed some sun. I felt as if I was in the wrong country. My parents went back home after bringing us all up in England. They got tired and said they needed home. Now, at nights I felt homesick for this country I had only ever been in four times, yet I wondered if I might feel more comfortable there, less visible. All of a sudden I felt lost, alone.

That night I suggested we all go on our family holiday the same as usual for two weeks in the summer. A holiday shared between us might act as some kind of miraculous cure. If we could just get back to those slow evenings when the children had just met new friends and were playing table tennis or cards, or having their Cokes and crisps and we were by the bar sitting on two tall stools, sipping a margarita with frosted salt, a little sunburnt, then our love would come back, spinning like one of the children's Frisbees on the long white sands. The idea of a holiday didn't go down well. She said, 'Actually I wanted to tell you that I'm going to be going on holiday with L.' I had this strange singing at the side of my temples. A new kind of noise for me, a sort of buzzing. 'And who is going to look after the children?' I said. 'I'll take my two to my mother; you can do what you want with your two,' she said. Since her affair, the children had suddenly become my two and her two, not our four, which was probably preparation, subconscious preparation. 'And what are you going to tell your mother?' 'I'll tell her I need a break and that me and a good friend are going on holiday and that is all she needs to know.' She said this last part slowly and with double emphasis as if I were really very stupid – and that is all she needs to know.

I spent that evening, the whole of that evening, on

the Net looking for a holiday to coincide with hers. I decided my sons and I needed somewhere different, somewhere we had never been before. I picked The Gambia. It's called the smiling coast. We'd hire a canoe and slide slowly down a creek watching out for monitor lizards and rare birds. We would drink green tea in the old market. We would meet a hundred-year-old crocodile called Charlie who shakes people's hands. I read all this out to my sons, the three of us crowded round my computer as I clicked on hotels. Both my sons were excited about this holiday, though surprised we weren't all going together. Children are good at making you feel positive about things. I imagined this new arrangement of ours might have some advantages. Solomon hugged me and said, 'Mum, we've never been on holiday just with you.' I booked it up; it was expensive, but I thought to myself, You only live once, you know?

I took a while that night putting my moisturizer on before getting into bed with her. We still slept the night together in the same bed because she said she didn't want the children getting suspicious. She had a firm belief in what she called Need to Know. Do they need to know? No. Do our parents need to know? No. It is none of anybody's business, she'd say. 'The more I think about it the more ridiculous marriage is. What a nonsense institution. We should lead the way. We should be like the Bloomsbury set. Why should any of us be conventional? Why should we all buy into this heterosexual model?' I wanted to agree. I tried to get the best part of myself to agree with her. Maybe it would have helped if I felt she still loved me too. Didn't they all love each other, that Bloomsbury set?

I found it hard to sleep next to her now – though she seemed to have no problem at all: out like a light, off to her dreams of L, lying on her back, on a lilo it seemed, drifting pleasantly out to sea. I had seen this L on a couple of occasions. She looked to me like any suburban housewife. Actually she looked like something out of *American Beauty* or *Desperate Housewives*. She had hair that was too done, silly-looking, and she was too white. She was red-haired. She was married. She was just the opposite of me. White and red-haired and tall. I think I would have preferred it if she had gone for somebody I could see was beautiful, somebody really special. And L didn't seem all that bright either. She could barely string a sentence together. But I tried to be nice to her in my head. I told myself to stop being so ungenerous. I didn't want to be like everybody else. I wanted to try very hard and rise above it and bring out the best in myself. I wanted that for myself, not for her. Still, I would slip into thinking that L's bob looked ridiculous and her clothes were sartorial mistakes and her eyes a bit vacant and so on. But everybody does this, surely? Criticizes the new lover because they feel so criticized themselves? It was my eyes that were vacant, my clothes that looked ridiculous, my hair that was silly. I mean what was I trying to do with my hair really? It was me that could no longer string a sentence together. It was me that couldn't concentrate enough to read a book.

I told her I had booked a holiday for Sol and Miles and me in The Gambia, and she said, 'Oh lovely!' and looked genuinely pleased for me. I don't know why I didn't like that reaction. It ate away at me all evening as we watched *Body Heat* together. I now found it very embarrassing to watch any film with sex in it with her. She didn't seem to mind. I could see that she wasn't thinking of me at all. She laughed out loud at bits of it and seemed to see the whole film as high camp and not as a dark film noir. She sipped away on her wine, enjoying herself. I was staring straight at the television and must have hopefully given the impression that I was watching it when all of a sudden I noticed a pile of her laundry on the sofa. On the top of the pile, as clear as anything, were a couple of pairs of thongs. I stared at these, dumbstruck, as the pair in *Body Heat* botched the killing of the husband. The music in my head was the music in theirs. She had never, ever worn anything like these for me. Never in all our fifteen years. For a while back in the beginning of our relationship when we were passionate and couldn't take our hands off each other she wore silk knickers a few times for me and fancy bras. But after six months it was Marks and Spencer's high-waist black pants, five to a pack. Not even bikini-style. What hurt me was not just the fact that she was clearly having different sex altogether with L, on the evidence of the thongs alone, but that she could just leave them lying casually like that on the top of her pile of washing without giving it a second thought.

I closed my eyes and pretended to snooze on the couch because I didn't want her to see the tears that had started rolling underneath my eyelids. I didn't want to be getting emotional and making a fuss. I wanted to get through this time, like you get through an operation, for my stitches soon to dissolve, for me to soon be past the not carrying anything too heavy stage, for me to be back on my feet again in say three or four months' time. I wanted to keep my head down.

When I opened my eyes, the tears had gone. She looked over at me and said quite affectionately, 'Did you have a little snooze? Doesn't it make you feel safe to have a little snooze in the middle of a movie?'

That night we got into bed about eleven o'clock. I had drunk more wine than usual. I had knocked back at least four glasses of a South African red. I stumbled up the stairs hoping that sleep would claim me before it claimed her. I put my head on the pillow and turned to face the window. I could see a tiny slice of sky where the curtains hadn't been closed properly. I could see two stars. I lay in the dark with her snoring behind me. Finally, unable to take any more, and dripping with sweat, I got up and put on the bedside lamp. She didn't even stir. I pulled open her underwear drawer. We never shared clothes or underwear or anything. She thought it was sick to share clothes. She said that was the one thing she hated about being with a woman, the possibility, the expectation that you should share each other's clothes. I loved the idea of sharing clothes. When I looked into the drawer, I nearly passed out. There were at least fifteen pairs of thongs in there lying like thin vipers in amongst a nest of old knickers. I checked their labels, all bought at Bravissimo. I had noticed that shop in the town before and gone in once for a measuring. They don't use a tape. They use the bra you are wearing and work from that. I never bought one in there. They were shockingly expensive. I thought of all the years of nothing. The years of waiting and loving and hoping. The years of feeling inadequate and unattractive. The years of being faithful. The years of touching her back in the night, hoping she would turn around to me. And those thongs lying there like that were a slap in my face. I couldn't get over the thinness of them. I held one pair up in the semi-dark and stared at it. I felt like a mad woman. I could feel my dark eyes burning through them. Thongs are actually designed to fit right up your ass. I saw her lying on some bed with black thongs on and the suburban housewife pulling the thin bit to the side and stroking her ass. I saw the suburban housewife's face all flushed as she rode her, pulling the thongs back and forth quickly across her ass like a woman on a dark horse with a short whip. I saw the whole thing play out in front of my eyes when I had been so good, when I hadn't done that for the whole four months, when I had pushed all those thoughts away, when I had let none of them in. I stared into the drawer. Some were plain black silk. Some were pink. Some were floral. One pair had a tiny rosebud sewn onto the back at the very top of the thin bit. Some were lace. Some had matching bras. At least four had matching skimpy bras.

She makes that strange catching snore sound, like somebody has just caught a fish in their sleep, and it is on its way up to the harbour, when all of a sudden it slides off the hook and slips back down to the sea. I let out a sigh of relief. I don't want her to wake up and find me like this. I tell myself not to but I still do it. I feel myself rise from the drawer and go down the stairs in the dark to the kitchen. All of the children are sleeping. I turn on the kitchen light. The dog looks at me from her basket, as if to say, What are you doing up? The kitchen clock says three in the morning. I pour myself a glass of water and again tell myself not to do it. But I can't help myself. I have had enough. I feel humiliated. She didn't even try to hide them from me. She doesn't think I have any feelings at all. I get out the recently sharpened secateurs from the drawer. Just the day before yesterday, I spent a pleasant afternoon pruning the roses with them. I finish my glass of water and put it on the draining board. I climb the stairs gripping the implements in my hands. I feel grim. I feel like a murderer. I creep up the stairs quietly as possible. I am still a little drunk and I stumble when I get to the top landing. I stop and think and listen. I say to myself, Only mad people do things like this and you are not a mad person. I say, Stop before you destroy everything. Then I open the drawer again and take the first pair of thongs out and cut off the tiny pink rosebud. I hesitate for a couple of heavy, still moments, then I cut the whole thong into tiny pieces, opening and closing the spring action of the secateurs, making sure the thong goes in the middle of the curve. The next pair is easier. The thin bit is so easy to cut through. The secateurs are bigger than the thongs. I feel ecstatic, high as a kite. I know what I am doing is wrong. There must be three hundred pounds' worth of thong here for Christ's sake, but it feels great. I feel free. I tell myself to do four pairs and leave the other eleven. But once I've started I can't stop. It is addictive, by the way, cutting up thongs. I whip myself up into a state of complete indignation. Look at it this way, I say to myself drunkenly, a pair for every year. Snip. Snip. Snip. Snip.

When I have finished I am completely exhausted. I climb back into bed and think of the worms we used to cut as children, how they kept wriggling after being cut, how they still seemed to be alive. I wonder if the thongs might find a way to piece themselves back together in the dark drawer during the night. I want to shake her awake and tell her we are finished. We are over. We are so finished. I lie there waiting for something to happen. The weather is clammy outside. The night air is close. My heart is thumping fast, as if I was running upstairs. I take deep breaths and try to breathe normally, in and out, in and out. I make a loud sound like a sighing sound. I turn around and lie on my back and put my hands behind my head. I lie staring at the rosebud light-fitting in our ceiling. It looks like icing on a cake. I feel drained, wretched about what I have done. She rolls over in her sleep and calls out her lover's name. I put my hands over my ears and try and fall asleep. At about five o'clock in the morning I finally do. I am hot, uncomfortably hot. I wake a little later when Hannah gets into bed with us. Hannah is eight. She comes in around half-past five every morning. She crawls between us. I watch her sweet rosy face as she falls back to sleep and think how much I will miss her.

In the morning, after she goes downstairs to make us a mug of green tea, I sit bolt upright and remember exactly what I have done. I feel frightened of myself and sick to my stomach. I don't want her to open her drawer and be confronted with the mad and revolting sight of all her special little knickers cut to shreds. She is nearly fifty; she was probably just trying to cheer herself up. I feel so sorry, so sorry. While she is in the kitchen, I get a plastic bag out of the bottom of the wardrobe and put all the shredded thongs into it. Later on I rush out to our garden and put them in the outside bin. There is one rose left still in bloom. There is nothing like the smell of an English rose. I bury my nose into it and breathe deeply. The petals are so soft, so impossibly soft.

Later that morning, I confess. It takes a while for me to form a sentence in my mouth that I can actually speak. 'Last night, I lost it a bit,' I say. 'How do you mean, lost it,' she says. 'Well, I got out the pruning scissors and cut all those new thongs of yours to ribbons.' She stares at me for a long time, then she makes this noise, a noise that sounds like Ugggghhhhh. She looks like she might collapse. I tell her I am sorry, I offer to go and buy her some new ones or give her, what, three hundred pounds?, to buy some new ones herself. She waves these suggestions away with her hands as if they revolt her. She looks at me, shocked, saddened, appalled. She says, 'I would never have believed it of you.'

Sonata

Perhaps all night trains have this air of the confessional, if two people find themselves in the right carriage, sleepless, watching small stations pass through them like waking dreams. I must have been watching you for a very long time, watching you without appearing to be interested in you at all. I knew we had a long night ahead of us; we had time. And I knew as soon as you opened your mouth that you had a story to tell and that your story would stretch across this troubled country of mine. It was a slow winter. Our journey through X and X and X had a surreal quality to it, as if we would never get to our destination, as if we would spend our lives on this night train, seeing the deep snow glow a little in the dark, the beautiful old lettering of some of our stations light up for a minute and then be gone.

I was staring into the night thinking that no one ever fathoms the dark. The dark is like a mirror. I could see only shapes in the night. I couldn't make them out.

You paused before you mentioned that this love you talked on and on about through the snow and through the small stations of X and X and X, through the thick, conspiratorial darkness, was a woman, and when you mentioned this you looked down into your furs and then looked quietly up again to see my expression. Your lashes blurred at the edges and you blinked prettily, as if you were saying, Are you surprised at this, that here I am this very pretty woman, and here this great love of mine is also a woman? They have an expression I heard used in England quite recently which made me laugh. (I have a loud laugh that is perhaps off-putting. I often try to dim it down.) The expression was *get over yourself*. I think this a good one for many reasons; perhaps all of the problems of the world are to do with the fact that we simply cannot, any of us, anywhere, get over ourselves.

English is not my language and it is not yours; so we could say, we shared English for the night as well. There is a certain camaraderie to be had from sharing a language that belongs to neither of you. You search for the right word; you appreciate what the other finds. The language becomes a kind of a dance; you take one step, I take the other. We both pronounce English differently, we emphasize the wrong part of a word just like beginners in Russian often don't get the sounds right. They never manage the B pronounced like the v of void or X close to the ch sound in the Scottish loch. Sometimes we forget perfectly ordinary words. You say to me, 'How do you call this green stuff?' and it takes me ten minutes to work out you mean grass.

Let me describe you because you are a woman who likes listening to descriptions of herself. How do I know this? I don't know. Only that I know it. You will smile prettily and your eyes will shine with self-delight. I have met women like you before.

You have very dark eyes that widen when something surprises you. You are demure. You have long eyelashes. You have beautiful bone structure. You look like a great beauty, like an actress. You have those kind of looks that make a stranger think they already know you because your beauty is classic. It is known. What is not known are your thoughts. Who ever heard the tormented thoughts of the great beauty? You have thick dark hair. You are wearing dark red lipstick. You are wearing a fur coat. Something in your expression tells me you have recently been having not a good time of it. I don't know what. But as soon as you opened your mouth, I knew that you wouldn't be able to stop, that you would be forced to tell me everything. And I would have to find some way to absolve you. We know things without knowing them.

You knew that your jealousy was a form of craziness, yet you walked towards it. You walked towards it in the pitch dark when all of your intelligence was saying stop. And so, how was it the poet put it? 'The heart that can no longer / Love passionately, must with fury hate.'

When I looked back on that journey with you, I knew I would be able to remember the exact moment your story began because I had been watching you, waiting for it to come. Strangers on the train can be so very intimate; this is true, is it not? We shared that night together and we will never meet again and yet, I don't want to sound melodramatic, for goodness' sake, I am a little pedantic, and the pedant hates melodrama, but it might not be an exaggeration to say that I felt something towards you that night like love. That journey will stay with me as proof that I am capable of profound intimacy. And yet I knew if I took your number that I would break the spell, that we could not ever repeat it. I think it was different for you than for me. I know you better than you know me. Isn't this always the way in relationships, that one person knows the other better?

Here is how you started. You leaned forward to me and you said, and it was a typical question but it didn't put me off, 'Do you know how long it will be before we reach X?' You spoke right away in English. I said, 'I'm not sure, the train seems to be running behind schedule, but it is so difficult to tell in the night.' You sighed. You were cold. I offered you my scarf and you took it, wrapping it round your neck. I cannot say what pleasure that gave me, watching you, such a great beauty, take my green scarf and wrap it round your neck. If I had known you better I might have asked you to do it again.

You sighed again and hugged yourself. Then you said, 'Do you think if you tell somebody something you still do not believe yourself, that it would help you to believe it?' I nodded. I was uncertain I wanted to hear what you clearly wanted to tell me. Part of me was enjoying sitting opposite you, making you up to myself. I wasn't sure I wanted you to come suddenly alive, to do your own thing. But I nodded because we were two people in the same carriage on a long night journey through the snow and what kind of human being would I be if I could simply not bear to listen? What is the cost of listening, do you think? And why are some people what they call good listeners and other people talkers? And how come talkers never get to be good? I wondered if being a good listener was really such a virtue. I am a terrible cynic because I have been betrayed so many times. Yet I am somebody who is a good listener.

During these hours of our journey, I got up a few times and fetched us a glass of tea from the buffet car. Once we had a vodka at three in the morning. That was the best potato vodka of my life, shared with you while you shared your life with me. During your story, I interrupted little except to make the odd observation. You needed my full attention. Nobody has needed my attention like that before, ever. It was, how do they say, *full on*.

We were two women who lived very happily together in an apartment in the old part of town. We were discreet about our relationship. Many people mistook us for sisters because we were both good-looking and svelte, slim, and because we loved each other so much something about us became the same, the same.

We dressed similarly. We shared our undergarments. We held each other all night long. At first we had sex – lots and lots of sex, no, and then we had no sex, yes? It was as if we became too . . . much, too intimate to have it, too close to each other's skin. Not enough to separate us, mmmmmnnh? We became like family, each other's mother and father and sister. I don't know. Explain to me how this happens. How you can go from ripping each other's clothes off to a kiss like this?

You purse your lips and kiss the cold night air.

And why this is. Is it because each of us is frightened of closeness sexually, and can only maintain it for a short period? I don't know. It's complex, no?

We worked at similar jobs. We loved our work and we could share that totally. We were a little competitive but we never admitted this to each other. This was another problem, that we were rivals like siblings can be rivals in the most awful way, whilst pretending to be each other's, how do you say, support, leaning on each other? We had to rely on each other a lot. There were not many people that we knew in Zagreb like us. I could have died for her. I could have put my hand beside my heart and promised to be with her when she was old – even when her skin was wrinkled and her teeth were not her own any more. Supposing she had been taken ill? I could have put my hand beside my heart and sworn to look after her, to take a cold flannel to her hot forehead, to wash her feet, to change her sheets. I often imagined this, is that strange, don't you think? I don't know why. But I imagined looking after her if she was ill. In my head maybe it was a test of love, because there are things about illness which I find revolting.

And it is strange now to look back on that time and to see how certain I felt about the future, about becoming an old woman, with her. I could have bet good money in the casino that we would be being together forever. Anything else was an outrage. Of course occasionally we would have arguments and at those times we would get very hard and upset and both of our hearts would hurt. But we never went to sleep without making things a little better. Usually it was with me saying sorry, sorry, sorry, yes? Usually at least three times to make it work properly – like a spell.

And then one morning, I got up and smiled at her and kissed her cheek and she got up out of bed very quickly. She said she had to hurry and that she was late for work and that was the last time I ever kissed her cheek in the morning. That night she came home with things from the delicatessen and left me some cheese, some chorizo, an artichoke, some olives, and a large red tomato on a white plate and said she was taking hers to her study to continue working. I ate the artichoke heart, which wasn't very tasteful, then threw the rest in the bin. It was so unusual for us not to eat together. I felt sick in the stomach.

At this point an old man came into our carriage and sat down. He was wearing a thick coat and a big fur hat. He took off his hat and nodded to us and lit his pipe. Then he said in my language, 'A very cold night, is it not? The train is running late. So much snow on the tracks.' I spoke with him a little. I was impatient to get back to you. I knew you might not speak now. 'How far are you going?' I asked him. He said he was only going as far as X. I looked at you and you looked at me back as if to say, Of course I can wait till X. You got up and went to the toilet and I missed you while you were gone. I had such a strong sense of our time being so short that I didn't want a single moment of it wasted. I never experienced this before. Actually quite the opposite. I am usually one of those people who discourages the train conversation, where are you going, who to see, for how long, etc. I never have interesting answers for a start. I am not usually visiting anybody. Of course I am a hopeless neurotic and I say this only for you to realize how unusual it was, for me at least, to be so engrossed, so compelled, so open to you.

When you came back, I noticed that you had freshened up your hair, and it was now sitting on top of your head. You had redone your red lipstick. You looked pale and impatient. You looked vampire pale; your white face made your red lipstick all the more red.

The old man took you in and smiled at you. I could see that he was charmed by your beauty. The beautiful have so much easier a time of it than the ugly, don't you think? They get smiled at the whole time. Strangers offer them things. People notice the beautiful; the beautiful are constantly acknowledged. They get service at the drop of a hat, faster service in bars and restaurants than the ugly. If they are crossing a road, cars stop for them quicker. It is true, but only the ugly would notice it. You were used to being noticed. I suddenly realized, before you even told me the next part of your story, that what had cut you was not the betrayal, but the fact that you were used to being noticed. You were used to getting all of her attention. You were one of those people in the world who is good at getting attention. Some don't need it and some crave it and some go to childish lengths to procure it. This was it, surely, the person who had given you all of her attention for thirteen years suddenly turned off the light and you could not see your beautiful face any more. You needed her to give you your own reflection, I think? It was like you were travelling on a train in the dark.

The old man closed his eyes; then you closed your eyes; then I closed mine. And the three of us shared forty winks. Then the train shuddered into X and the old man rubbed his eyes. He climbed the steep steps onto the platform and I bent down and handed him his old, battered case. He thanked me warmly but looked at you. The beauty. Even though you didn't lift a beautiful finger to help the old man. Such is life. You see. I am used to the ways of it.

A younger man put his head through our carriage door and my heart sank. But he didn't like the trail of pipe tobacco the old man had left. You watched him

sniff the air and then walk on. I felt relief. So did you.
I could see it on your face, it swept across the plane of
your high cheeks. I sat down opposite you. Your head
was leaning against the window. You stared out at the
snow for some time. The train was still stationary and
we could see the snow better, lit up by the lights in the
station. It shone with the promise of oblivion. You got
out your silver cigarette case and took a cigarette from
it. You offered one to me. I shook my head but slipped
your silver lighter out of your hand, just as you were
about to light your cigarette, and lit it for you myself.
You breathed your smoke in deeply and exhaled,
blowing a thin, quick line of smoke out of the corner
of your mouth. You held the cigarette poised in your
hand. I thought perhaps that you were not going to tell
me any more. Your face looked troubled by too many
thoughts. The train started up again, its engine cough-
ing and spluttering in the cold. It juddered and for a
moment it sounded like the engine was going to fail
completely. Then it seemed to will itself into movement
and we took off again. It got darker and darker inside
our carriage.

That night I put the chorizo and cheese in the bin,
I heard her playing the piano in our living room. We
had a beautiful baby grand piano that had been lifted
into our apartment through the sash windows with a
crane. The day it arrived, all the neighbours gathered
around in the street outside and watched it being
pulled up into our front room like a great black bird.

It was such a special day. Everyone out in the street with their mouths open, yes, nobody spoke a single word, until the piano was safe and then people spontaneously clapped, as if we were all at the opera.

Her playing sounded different. It sounded out of control. She played a piece I had heard her play before, the Kreutzer Sonata, but this time she played it as if the demon were in her fingers. It made me feel fearful just to listen to it. It made me think of white dogs in the snow, of red meat. It made me think that something violent was going to happen to my life. I opened the door a little and watched her at the piano. I am not exaggerating. No, it is not too much to say she looked possessed, yes? She did not look well. Her long hair was hanging over her face. She usually put it up to play. Her face had such a strong look of concentration, she looked vicious. Not at all pretty any more. She was talking to herself fiercely as she played, counting, totally involved in the music. If a bomb had exploded at the end of the street she would have sat playing amongst the rubble. The skin on her face was tight with ambition. I looked down horrified at her foot, her foot pressing on the pedal of the piano with such precision, such poise, in her black leather shoes. Even the instep of her foot was rigidly tense, ready to pounce. It was as if the piano, which used to be a source of leisure and pleasure, had now become her prey. I closed the door quietly and went to bed early with my book. Can you believe it but I was rereading *Crime and*

Punishment? Even at night that summer it was too hot. The heat trapped you in your own home.

'This summer gone?' I interrupted her to ask.

Yes, this summer gone. Very humid. No breeze. No air. Our apartment was stifling, stuffy. I could feel the desire coming off her. I could feel it. It was revolting. I got out our fan and plugged it in. I could still feel her heat even as I imagined the fan lifting the sheets of music, and making them flutter, as if they were playing on their own. The music got in my head. I could not concentrate for it. It became the music of the end of our relationship, the music of our finale. I will never be able to listen to it again as long as I live. What a thing it is to have music that plays your terrible thoughts. I imagined that one piece could drive more delicate women than myself to insanity.

'Goodness,' I said, 'what a pity. I know that piece. It is a wonderful piece of music. Do you not think we should listen more objectively when we listen to music?'

'Perhaps,' you said, and looked out of the window, considering my question. 'Perhaps,' you said again, as if you actually might like to impress me. You rubbed your shoulders, cold still, and tightened my scarf around your neck. I could see your breath in the carriage. The heating was not working properly. I was annoyed at myself for interrupting you. You seemed to have left me to go back into your own world. Very still moments passed between us as the train slid through the middle of my country. I looked out of the window and thought how the near dark and the far-away dark are different colours. There was a half-moon in the sky. It had a blood-red glow around it. It looked as if it had been sliced cleanly down the middle with a butcher's knife.

She told me she was going to be playing the Kreutzer Sonata with Isadora, this new friend of hers, yes. She was excited because she said they had been asked to play at a charity concert. Am I stupid? Did she think I don't see what is laid before my eyes to see? Is she pretty, this Isadora? I asked her one night playing with her hair. She took my hand away. Don't do this, she said, it is irritating. You see it had got so crazy she didn't like my touch? Maybe, she said. Her eyes were shining with new light. She didn't even try and hide from me. So I asked her outright. I said, Are you in love with her? Have you fallen for her?

She looked completely shocked; actually she looked appalled. She said, Of course not. Don't be so silly. She is a friend and a fellow musician. I like how she plays the violin. You like how she plays the violin, I echoed because it sounded obscene to me. Yes, she repeated, very innocently, Yes, yes. I like how she plays the violin. It is that simple. She inspires me. I can learn a lot from her. She is really very good. Her timing is superb. Well, but now she was giving me too much detail. Yes, but, I said again. And is she pretty? Well, her looks are not the kind of looks I usually like, she said. She is too tall, blonde. She is not my type. I suppose to others she is pretty. And this did not console me, because she said *usually*. Looking back on it, all that I can think is that I knew before she knew. Perhaps, and this thought is horrible to me, perhaps I even opened her eyes to it by asking that question. Perhaps if I had never asked that question she would have never discovered it?

Anyway, I suppose I believed her that hot night. I told myself that this concert was very important to her and I must stop being so demanding. I tried to support her. I cooked her special little meals. But she would not eat them. I bought good red wine, but she only sipped at it. I bought her a new top, but she thought it didn't suit her. I tried everything. It was like she had fallen sick to me. She so much wanted to do her own thing that anything associated with me was to be pushed away. Like this.

You pushed violently in front of yourself.

I felt like I lived in a small apartment in the old part of town with a cold stranger now. My love, who used to spend every minute with me, was now shutting me out. She had somebody else who made her sparkle and shine. Even if she didn't know it. I knew it. I knew it. And so the day came when I could stand it no longer.

At this point our train pulled into X. Three young men wearing suits and carrying briefcases got into our carriage. They nodded at us. I could see that they thought we were together, maybe friends, because of the way they nodded at us as if we were one, not two. I liked that. It made me feel I belonged to somebody for even a short while. On that train journey across our country when our country was suffering all sorts of troubles and when this group were fighting that group, and nobody ever felt completely safe, not even at the opera or the theatre, especially not at the opera or the theatre, I thought to myself, it is possible to feel safe and contained by a stranger in a carriage on a train.

You rolled your eyes when the men came in. You looked at your watch. We still had three hours to go before we reached X. You closed your eyes. I worried that you would fall into a deep sleep and wake up only when we arrived. You looked so tired. You looked as if your story was taking it out of you. I was already considering giving you my number and saying something casual like, 'If you would like to finish telling me your story some other time, you could call me, and we could have a vodka or a grappa or a coffee or whatever . . .' Or something like, 'I have enjoyed being with you on this train so much. I have never had a lover for longer than a year but I think you are beautiful. I understand you completely. Will you meet me again?' Or something like, 'It was meant that we should be in this same carriage. We were meant to meet. You were meant to tell me this story. It is fate. What are we going to do next?' But I am a good listener and not a talker. In the dimming light of our carriage, I noticed your mouth, how full and sensuous it looked as you slept, how your bottom lip was slightly parted from your top one.

The men were men from Moscow and were obviously businessmen. They were talking about money. I never understand talk about money so I simply let the conversation fly over my head. The tall, handsome man's mobile went off in his pocket. He answered, talked for a bit, then I heard him say, 'That's the deal, take it or leave it. I don't know how many times I have to say this!' When he put down the phone, he shook his head, in a temper. 'It was my wife,' he said. 'We are in the middle of an acrimonious divorce.' The shorter man said, 'She rings you up in the middle of the night?'

'Oh yes. She specializes in the middle of the night. The sooner we settle it all the better. It is doing my head in.'

'There's a lot of money in divorce these days. Divorce is big business. It didn't used to be,' the third man said thoughtfully. His hair was black and greased down and he had a rather unappealing centre parting.

You shifted in your seat and snuggled into the side of the carriage. I wondered how my language sounded to you, how much of it you understood. 'Friends of mine from New York paid a lawyer a massive amount in a costly, bitter divorce. They even went to court over their dog, who should get custody of the dog, can you believe that?' the centre-parting man said.

'We don't have a dog or children,' the handsome

man said. 'Our problem is we never had enough to share. In the end we just had absolutely nothing in common: zilch.'

I shifted in my seat and looked at you. You had opened your eyes and were staring out of the window again. And then the train pulled into X and the three men got out. They had taken with them half an hour of my story. My eyes burnt holes into their backs. At this point, I still had no idea, absolutely no idea how far your story was going to go. I just knew that you had me hooked, perhaps for my own private reasons.

I was tired. My eyes felt sore from looking into the dark and trying to fathom it. Your voice was now inside my head. It seemed to go with the snow and the dark, your deep, husky, smoker's voice. You halted often, straining to use a language that was not natural for you. This I found sexy, the stopping and the starting. Your voice was like the train. Whenever I go on that same journey again, I think I can hear it under the sound of the wheels on the tracks. It is the particular rhythm of somebody who is not speaking in their mother tongue, though both of us are more fluent in English perhaps than some that live there. I have a friend in London. These days when I ring him to ask him what he is doing he says, 'Just chilling,' and it is so annoying because he rarely says more than that. Perhaps he no longer welcomes my calls. The train is still stationary. I notice you only ever start talking when it moves off, as if you need the sound of the engine or the movement to tell your story. You looked at me and arched your eyebrows and looked at your watch again. Something had changed in the way you told your story now; you seemed reluctant to get back to it, as if you couldn't face it any longer. You gave me the impression that you might just abandon it altogether and fall as silent as the faithful snow outside.

During this period I actually feel as if some part of myself has been banished to another part of the world. I feel as if I cannot live my life to the full and feel everything I am capable of feeling unless I have this love. The pleasure goes from me; the delight goes. Nothing means anything. I am dulled at my edges. I have a weight across my chest that is as heavy and as surprisingly soft as a snake. I am sure that the weight is the weight of my broken heart. Two pieces of heart weigh more than one. I feel for the first time in my life that life and love are the same thing; without love you have no life. She feels for the first time that passion and life are the same thing. I see it on her cheeks, in her eyes, in the way she moves, in the fact she starts to go on a diet, and in the way she grows her hair and in the different clothes she buys. If she cannot see it, she is a fool. But I see it. But I have no proof. Some part of me says to myself, You don't want to find such proof. But the other part says, Prove that she is a liar. And so I go hunting for the truth. And this is the how do you say it, when the road goes like this.

You join your wrists together and hold your beautiful hands apart.

'The fork in the road?' I say.

There is another expression I like better than this one.

'The crossroad?' I say.

Exactly. Yes. The crossroad. This is when I could have gone another way but I didn't. And I know it in my own head. I say, Don't do this. You are the one that will pick up the bill for this. Leave her to have her little excitement, she will come back to you when she is finished because you know her like nobody else. You love her like nobody else. Let her have her silly bit of adolescent passion. She has bought for herself some very silly clothes. Not her. They just do not suit her style. I say all this to myself, I talk to myself in a heavily emphasized way. I have lost all my subtlety, all my dignity, all my grace. My head gives me no peace. How can she do this. How can she become this stranger. Has she forgotten herself. Has she forgotten everything we had. Did we ever have what I thought we had and so on. It is non-stop. It follows me everywhere, my own voice like a dog, like a thin dog looking for where it buried the bone. It goes to sleep with me. It wakes up with me. I am raging. I am lost. I look at her sleeping in these days. She sleeps the night away till she can wake and be with her love. She is closed to me even in her sleep.

And so I open up the drawer where I know she keeps her special things and in that drawer what do you suppose I find?

At this point the guard comes in to inspect our tickets. I never understand why a ticket needs to be inspected more than once on the journey. He looks at you closely as he takes your ticket as if he recognizes you, as if he thinks you are a great actress. You put your ticket away in your purse and smile tightly at him. He nods. You nod back. He is a cursory guard; someone who would like to have even more power, I suspect, than his job allows, someone who would really like to put the fear of God into people. He examines me, suspiciously, as if I have cheated him out of something. He takes my ticket and looks at it for a long time. I wonder if there is something wrong with my ticket. He says, 'So you are travelling all the way to X? It is a long journey.' 'Yes,' I say, stumped for anything more to say. 'It is.' The guard nods silently and goes on his way.

I find nothing. I don't know what I expected to find, evidence of some kind, but there are no love letters there, no photographs, no bits of paper with telephone numbers on it, nothing. And yet still, I know it. I know it in my bones. This jealousy is already singing its mean little song to me, like a childhood taunt. I am reduced by it. By day I feel myself grow small. I look in the mirror and my skin looks dull. The thoughts in my head are not so interesting any more because I have no one to share them with. I try to do certain pathetic things to make myself feel better. I wear high heels because this woman is tall. I have my hair shaped by a very expensive hairdresser. And though she notices some of these things, she seems not at all interested in me any more. She looks at me and sometimes says, 'Your hair is nice,' or some such compliment but she cares nothing, nothing. She speaks like an automaton now. Her mind is far away. I feel how distant she is when she is standing close to me. She could be on the other side of the mountain. There is a mountain air that comes off her radiant cheeks, a fresh, scented air as if she has been to some special place that I have not; even when we have both spent the whole day together, I feel this. The truth is she has a life without me, when she used to share the thoughts inside her head. I can feel it, this inside-life that she has. It always places me far away on the outside. It makes me lonely. It makes me, how do you say it, nostalgic for my own past. It makes me homesick while I am still at home.

One time she comes home with this look on her face. How shall I call that look? A certain smugness. I say to her, 'We never make love any more, why don't we?' And she says, 'It has been such a long time that we can't just rush into it. We need to take our time.' 'Take our time?' I say. 'It has been years.' But conversations such as that always pass with no satisfactory outcome. Somehow she just slips out or under them and before I know it we are talking about something else.

You get your cigarettes out and light one and blow out the smoke. Though I have never smoked myself, I don't mind it when you do. You only notice your ash when it becomes quite long, you catch it in the nick of time and flick it into the ashtray at the side of your seat. You manage to look attractive doing this. I can hardly believe what I am hearing. I have never spoken to a more perfect creature. You are beautiful – beautiful and tormented and intelligent and sensitive. It is incomprehensible that someone should not desire you. Goodness, they should be so lucky. I want to lean towards you and kiss your cheek but of course someone like you would never look at someone like me. I am not good-looking enough. I am clumsy, big-boned. Of course I have fine tastes, but having fine tastes is of no use to one if one is big-boned. At the end of the day you still have a large hand around a dainty teacup and it is off-putting, it is not a big draw.

And what is more from the way that you are telling me this story, I can tell that you would not even consider finding me attractive. Perhaps jealousy is not at all what one feels for somebody else, perhaps jealousy is all about what one feels for oneself. Even the beautiful are fragile, I take comfort from this. Perhaps the beautiful are even more fragile because they are beautiful. Perhaps the ugly are less breakable, tougher, happier to be loved at all. We break the world up into opposing groups the whole time, the rich and the poor, the young and the old, the black and the white, men and women, but actually as far as I can see the most neglected difference is between the beautiful and the ugly. The ugly have no rights. They don't even feel the right to be loved. They feel grateful for the simplest of kindnesses, such as someone saying thank you or please or someone holding a door open. Actually we feel grateful to be spoken to, to be taken seriously. You look out of the window. You have lapsed into one of your small silences. I look out of the window too. I cannot believe how endless the snow is during our winters, how implacably there it is, as if it will never, ever melt. The land underneath the thick snow is a secret, a secret months old.

We still slept in the same bed together during this time. I didn't sleep so well any more. I counselled the dark. Sometimes she fell thickly asleep only to wake me up as she laughed and giggled like a maniac in her sleep. When I heard that laughter I knew for definite she was in love. I asked my doctor. She said, Laughing in one's sleep is a sign of being in love. It scared the living daylights out of me. The next morning, I said to her, You were laughing in your sleep. And she looked undressed by me. Then she said, Oh for goodness' sake, leave me alone. Give me some peace. I am tired of being watched. You are making me feel jumpy in my own house. Stop watching my every move or you will finish us off! Watching your every move? I said. What nonsense. You were laughing loudly, hysterically in your sleep. Like this. Hee Heee Heeeee, Ha Ha Ha!

You woke me up. That is all. I am not sitting awake watching you sleep, for goodness' sake. You woke me up! Yes, yes, yes, she said. But still, you know what I mean. It is not just then. It is all the time. You are constantly watching me. I feel it.

I am not, I said to her – though of course there was a little truth in what she was saying – I am merely noticing all these sudden changes in you. How can I not notice when they feel like such a rejection?

Oh, stop going on about rejection, she said. It is not sexy. It is so boring. No wonder people that rant on about being rejected get rejected. Leave me alone. Give me some peace.

I wondered if she was being so horrible to me because she felt guilty about betraying me. Or if she just didn't like me any more. She made me feel so disliked. Actually, I felt she was contemptuous of me. She had gone from thinking I was the most important person in her life to treating me like an annoying little cousin that has been sent from Constanta to stay the summer in Bucharest, some little runny-nosed child. Not me. She was not seeing me any more. She had some other impression of me in her head and I couldn't correct it. I couldn't get to what it was. I kept wanting to say, Anna, this is me. This is me, your love. How can you forget me so quickly? How can you cast me in this role?

A thought occurred to me as she was talking. It struck me with force. I could tell that she was a private person, that she was not used to telling strangers her intimate business, why had she picked me? That was the first thought and the second thought was, given that her confidence had been so diminished by this raging jealousy, how come she felt more than confident to tell me the whole story, without once ever saying, even out of politeness, Am I boring you, Is this going on too long, Are you still interested in my story, or even, Do you believe me? What gave her the right to tell the story to me in such painstaking detail; what made her think it was interesting to me? Did she see me and suspect that I had similar tendencies? Certain parts of her story did not tally. I did not believe she had gone and asked her doctor about the laughter in the sleep. I excused myself for a moment and told her I had to go to the bathroom. I went to the bathroom and took a good look at myself in the mirror. What had I had by way of lovers? How was I qualified to even understand the complexities that I was hearing? What if her entire story was made up and she had picked me to make a fool of me? Did I believe her every word? Did it matter what I believed? I washed my face with cold water and combed my hair. The train had just pulled into X. I got off the train and went to the buffet on the platform. I bought us both a glass of tea. I came back, handed her the glass of tea, which she took in a distracted way, not noticing really what I was giving her. I felt myself grow a little impatient with her. Yes, yes, I know – the traumatized are monstrously self-obsessed. Whatever she has done has so shocked her that she cannot come out of herself to even notice a stranger bringing her a glass of lemon tea. What do I owe this stranger? I owe her precisely nothing. I have already given her too much. I have listened for nearly six hours now. I have bought her a very good vodka, and two glasses of tea. What is the matter with me? Am I so flattered by the attentions of a pretty woman that I will do anything? If I asked her to close her eyes and describe me, I would not be surprised if she could not manage it. In a way, she is talking to the dark. In a way, I am her mirror.

You look straight at me for a second as if contemplating me. You look as if you are reading my thoughts. I feel a little unnerved by the frankness of your stare. Then you say quietly, in your deep, sexy voice, 'Thank you for the tea.' The smile on my face is perhaps too large. I say, 'Oh, it is nothing. You are very welcome.'

So one day I thought to myself: enough, I am fearing this woman I have never seen. I am making things up to myself. If only I could see her, then I would know for sure. That evening – a rare evening of calm between us, something had settled and it seemed as if we could live on with this familiarity, this thing that was not passion any more, but was still caring – I suggested something. I knew she didn't want to leave me. Otherwise, she would have left already, no? I knew I was her security. She still needed me. She needed to come home to our home and sleep in our bed and play her piano. She was too much of a coward to simply say,

I am sorry I have fallen in love. We must divide. And for my part, though I was not contented, I thought, I cannot imagine my life without her. Anna is my life. I must try and adapt and cope with her changes and maybe good things will come of these changes. Maybe somebody somewhere will reward me for my perseverance.

So I said to her that night, Perhaps we should have a few friends around and you should practise your sonata with Isadora and they can hear you play? It would be a dress rehearsal, no? We could have some food, some wine, some music. It has been so long since we had company. She looked at me a little suspiciously at first as if trying to find some other motive. Then her face broke into a smile and she kissed me for the first time in ages on my cheek.

You touch your cheek quite theatrically.

Well, thank you, Esther, she said. I think it is a good idea.

A few weeks later we had ten friends round. I had ordered and prepared the food and tidied our apartment, which was always very tidy in any case. Anna put on a beautiful new dark red dress and she looked quite lovely. I felt a stab of desire for her just like I had in the beginning of our love. Her cheeks were flushed and pretty and she had the look of a woman who is in love. I felt shut out from it. I felt a little dismayed. There she was looking the best I had seen her look for ages and it was nothing to do with me. For a moment

I was cross with myself for feeling like this. After all, we do not own people; we cannot own them. What is monogamy but a desire to possess somebody completely? Even their beauty has to be yours. That night her beauty felt such a private thing; it was between her and her love. I felt I was interrupting things even to notice it as fully as I did. I too was wearing a new dress.

Our friends arrived and everybody was sitting talking and drinking quite merrily when Isadora walked into the room. I didn't think her so very beautiful but as soon as she walked in I saw Anna's eyes light up and her cheeks grow even more flushed. I decided I had to take control of the situation by being very friendly towards Isadora. I said, Isadora, how lovely to meet you at last, I have heard so much about you. Anna has really been enjoying playing with you. She is so excited about this concert that you are going to be doing. Isadora was friendly back to me, but a little uncomfortable. She looked as if she had made the wrong decision and actually wanted to be somewhere else. She nodded and said she too was looking forward and then she looked around the room as if asking for help.

After the food and the wine, we went into the room with the baby grand piano and Isadora started tuning her violin. She looked so concentrated as she did it, even slightly bad-tempered. I noticed her arms looked strong. I noticed she had a bruise under her chin where her violin rested, quite a dark bruise the size of a plum. I noticed the beautiful colour of her violin, a rich orange-blossom wood. Anna sat down at the piano and together they started to play the sonata. The room filled with the sound of their music. They smiled at each other as they were playing like two people that were passing some important, some crucial, some life-or-death secret between them. Like two people that had always known each other, since they were small girls. Like two people who would know each other when they were old women. I was powerless in front of the spectacle of their love. I felt sick to watch it and at the same time kept this composed smile on my face. My face tilted to the side in appreciation of their high art. They played the piece to the end. All the time the music was playing it took me to unbearable places: I forgot myself, then remembered myself, then forgot again. I felt the music strip me of everything I ever owned, everything I ever loved. Outside the sky darkened and it started to rain. The sound of the stormy rain mixed with their music, made it even more intense. And all of a sudden, I felt so alone, so completely alone in a room full of admiring people. I wondered if our friends could see what I could see – that Isadora and Anna were meant for each other.

After the piece had finished, I went to my bathroom and stared at myself in the mirror. I felt like I was climbing down the stairs of my love, and that when I got to the bottom I would be lost. I could no longer tell myself that I was imagining things. It was plain to me. Now all I had to do was decide what to do and when to leave. And if I had just simply enjoyed the concert and congratulated them and allowed them to enjoy this time together, it would have all been very different, for me at least.

It is very dark now and your voice has become very low like the lowering dark. It has become one with the land outside the window, mysterious and untouchable, and remote. And because it is so remote it is the most intimate sound I have ever heard. I want to stop you now. I want to say, Whatever you did, I forgive you. Don't tire yourself out telling me any more now. Let us just enjoy this journey in the dark together. Let us have no more words. Your face is in shadows. You are hunched up into yourself. I can barely make you out. The train stops at another station. We have only one hour before we reach our destination. My mind is racing, trying to think ahead to how you might have ended things. I don't imagine you feel anything for me very much. But I have noticed the way you move your hands when you talk, the way you push some strands of your hair away from your face, the way you cross and uncross your legs. In this carriage with you, I could continue, across our troubled country for a very long time. I would like to pull a blanket down from above and wrap it around your lovely shoulders and tuck you up. Then I would like to kiss your cheek. And I would like to be bold enough to say, It is as well all this happened because you were meant to meet me and I would never betray you. I love the sound of your voice.

I love the way you close your eyes when you are trying to think of a word. I love the way you tell a story. Could you, perhaps, love somebody like me? Somebody who has no grace, who is big-boned and clumsy, but somebody who appreciates every fine thing in life and will give you only fine things ever and will only ever treat you as you deserve to be treated? I can see that you are a woman of delicate tastes.

You close your eyes for a moment. I can tell you are getting to the difficult bit of your story. I am not sure I want to hear it. You are still perfect to me. Everything you have said so far I can understand. I am still with you. I don't want you to say something that will make me part company with you. I don't want you to be crazy. I feel as if I have known you for a very long time.

But there is nothing I can do to stop you. You sigh and tears roll down your cheeks and you say to me simply, tired of the details, I couldn't take any more. When Isadora left that night I confronted my Anna. I said to her, It was so obvious that you love her. I am sure everybody in the room saw. Why won't you simply be honest with me and tell me the truth? She stared at me very surprised and she said, You make up so much in your head. I don't know you any more, Esther. I want us to separate. I can't live with this kind of suspicion. It is killing me. It has already killed us. You have made yourself up this long and elaborate story because you have fallen out of love with me. I gave out an incredulous gasp at this point. Yes, she said, it is you who have tired of me. You are simply needing me to do it. Very well. I will break it off. Enough. Enough, Esther! I have had enough! And she picked up a paperweight and hurled it across the room. It narrowly missed me. I ran at her and grabbed her by her shoulders and screamed at her, How dare you make me think I am going mad when you know very well you love her. How dare you? I slapped her straight across the face. I felt thrilled to be at last able to act decisively. I whipped myself up into a state of absolute dejected fury and it felt better than the lonely quiet times I had had. So much better. I slapped her again. I said to her coldly, I hate you. Get out. Get out of my life. She went to our bedroom and pulled down the suitcase from the top of the wardrobe and started packing. She was crying more out of indignation than anything else. I would never have believed this of you, Esther, she said. That you could act so crazy. I am not safe around you. I never meant to hurt you. I only ever meant to love you. Who knows where it goes to, this love, when it goes. Who knows where it goes? She said this sadly, to herself, shaking her head. She was packing quickly as she spoke. It was the most open she had spoken to me for months. I was startled for a moment then the rage came back even worse. I looked at the back of her head and hated the shape of it.

So you admit it has gone after all, I said nastily. You have made it go, she said. You and your crazy jealousy and your imaginings. Isadora would never go with a woman. She is happily married with two children.

She looked so self-righteous when she said this, as if nobody had ever heard of a married woman going off with another woman.

Well, she packed up and she left that night. I ripped the curtains off the windows and threw them out into the street as she got in a taxi. I screamed, Take these. They are your curtains. But of course she didn't take them.

All night that night, anybody could have stared into my apartment. She looked up at me and she waved and I will never forget that wave of hers as long as I live. Three months later she was dead. I never saw her again.

I sit forward in my seat. I am alarmed. I had not expected the story to finish like this and I am devastated. What do you mean, dead, I say like an idiot.

I am tired speaking in English, you say. My own language is mixing up with it and I am exhausted. Too many sounds in my head.

Yes, but what do you mean dead, I say again. What do you mean. How did she die?

You speak very slowly, thickly, as if there is fur in your mouth. Your voice is flat. I imagine you outside the train wading through the deep, thick snow, alone. You are so cold. You are shivering. I cannot believe she is dead.

She had cancer. She had a very fast cancer that swept

through her body and took her very quickly. She never told me. Nobody did. She didn't want to see me again. Then a couple of days before she died, I got a card from her, that told me nothing about her being ill but simply asked if I would come and visit her in her new place. I wrote back saying should I expect to see Isadora there too? And a few days after that I got a call from a mutual friend that told me Anna was dead.

And it was too late for me. It was too late for my jealousy. It was too late for everything. You cannot turn the clock back when somebody dies. You are consigned to always turning it forward and to seeing the bleak years stretch out ahead of you like the snow thinking if only, if only, if only. The future is endless when someone dies; you have years and years of not them, years to get through your life as best as you can. And what does it all matter, those petty jealousies compared to a life, to a love, what does it matter. Jealousy is as cruel and as cold as the snow. It bites, it takes you out, it gets you lost. You can never return from jealousy. Once you have gone there, you cannot get back. You cannot come back the same way.

I try and comfort you for you are really crying now. Well, I say, you weren't to know. I go over to your side of the carriage and put my arm around you. I hold you tightly. I say, There, there, hush, but you weren't to know, hush, hush, hush. All you did was love too fiercely.

And now I think, maybe she could feel it, this

illness inside her. Maybe that was the passion. Maybe the passion was death, the passion was that she had to play that one piece of music brilliantly before she died and I spoiled it. I will never, ever be able to forgive myself. Never. I loved her. I will never love again like that. And she never got to play in that concert with Isadora. She died a few days before the concert was supposed to happen.

You sob now, out loud on the train. The guard walks by outside in the corridor and stops for a second, listens, then walks on. 'I might as well have killed her.'

I forgive you, I say. I forgive you. I recite some Latin remembered from school days. In nomino nomina nominas padre, madre, some nonsense cobbled up but soothing-sounding, padre, madre, nomino nomina, dulce et decorum est pro patria mori. I have reverted to war poetry now. You hold both my cheeks in your hands and through your tears you say, Thank you, thank you, and you kiss the tears from my face and then you kiss my lips briefly. You take off my green scarf and go to hand it back to me. Keep it, I say to you. Please, I would like you to have it.

You wrap it around your beautiful neck.

And then our train reaches its destination. I have been dreading it would get there and knowing that it would, knowing that arrival was inevitable, unavoidable. How bizarre, I think to myself, to be on a train and to actually not want to arrive anywhere? What kind of madness is that? I get your suitcase down from the luggage rack and I pull my small bag down as well. I climb down the steep steps of the train then I help you down too. You seem weak from all your talking.

We walk along the platform very slowly together, like people that have suddenly become old together on the course of a single journey. We walk side by side in silence. I don't know if you dread parting like I do. You have stopped talking altogether. We pass through the station. I imagine what we look like from above. Two trusting people with their luggage walking slowly through the station after a long, long journey. I think of asking you for your address, for your phone number. I think of saying, It would be so lovely to keep in touch, would it not. I try and pluck up the courage to say this one simple sentence as we wait together in the taxi queue.

I think about how lonely Anna would have felt dying without her love. I think about why she didn't contact you sooner. I think about pride, how pride distorts and demeans. It is freezing cold. The temperature must be minus fifteen. The air crackles. The skin on my face tightens. The taxi queue grows inevitably shorter and we reach the front too fast. Again I have the terrible feeling of not wanting to get to the front of the queue, not wanting to leave you. You look round at me for a second as though you are going to say something. And all of a sudden you are climbing into your taxi and I am holding your door open before I get into mine. All of a sudden I am opening the door of my taxi and suppressing the desire to simply say, Follow that taxi. I don't know what to do with myself. I sit as close as I can to the window.

Our taxis travel together up the steep short road from the station. We stop at a red traffic light together. I am looking into the back of your taxi. I have no idea where it is heading for. Then it happens, the thing happens, your taxi turns to the left and mine turns to the right and I turn round frantically and wave at you out of the back window and you wave at me swivelling round too. I can see my green scarf wrapped round your lovely neck. You keep your hand pressed to the back window of your taxi. I take my hand and press it to the window of mine. Our hands are like our train stopped at the station.

The mirrored twins

Hamish and Don set out on a Saturday morning in November first thing; they had on their navy-blue waterproof jackets and jeans and their boots. They didn't leave a route behind with anybody because neither of them was that kind of man. Each man had a rucksack on his back. Inside Hamish's were ham pieces and jelly pieces, a bottle of water, a tiny flask of whisky and a bar of tablet, two Mackintosh red apples, two cans of McEwan's, a tin of mince and a tin of peas. Inside Don's were a bar of chocolate, four pieces of fruit, matches, two plastic bowls and spoons, two toothbrushes, toothpaste, a flask of sugary tea, two pairs of spare boxers. It had taken them years to find each other. Hamish was fifty-seven and Don was forty-nine.

They planned to drive past Balquhidder and start their walk by the picnic spot just beyond Loch Doine, to do a six-hour circuit walk and then do another the following day, staying in the bothies that you find for walkers along the way. Both men had been in climbing groups years ago. Hamish's climbing group had gone to New Zealand from Glasgow to Southampton by train and then by boat down the Bay of Biscay, into

the port of Wellington in seven weeks. They'd polished
off serious walks like the Routeburn track long before
it ever became easy, before the route was mapped out
for people, made toffee. They'd done it in the savage
days when you really could have got lost in the bush
and never have been seen again. Hamish met his wife
in New Zealand, fell in love had two children, plodded
along for ten years, then his wife left him which seemed
like a calamity at the time, but turned out, two years
later, not to be a calamity at all, but a liberation.

Hamish and Don knew the mountains and the hills
of Scotland as intimately as they knew people, even
more intimately perhaps. They knew the Cobbler and
his wife, the fine boulders of Crauch Ardrain; the great
views into the Arrochar Alps from the summit of Ben
Vorlich exhilarated them. The little hills, the Lomond
Hills, the Mamlorn Hills, the Glen Lyon Horseshoe,
the Secluded Glen over the two peaks at the edge of
the howling, lonely Rannoch Moor – all of it felt as
if it was mapped out on their own bodies. So familiar
– the good ridges and the old settlements, the cairns
and the rocky peaks, the grassy slopes, the serious
ascents, the wild descents. They enjoyed an entertaining ascent, a good challenge in their hard hiking boots.

It pleased Hamish and Don that they had a climbing past in common. It felt sometimes to Hamish that
he had climbed a very difficult mountain to find Don
at the summit, his face rugged, his skin mountain-
fresh, his hair thick as gorse.

Now it seemed all the climbing groups had gone, those big bands of boys that roamed the world and climbed the mountaintops. People did these things more and more on their own now, as if there was some sort of virtue in doing things solo, reaching a famed and favoured destination with no assistance whatsoever in the fastest time possible. All the pleasure had gone out of the big group and nobody seemed to talk politics any more, not in the same way anyway. Where were the men now you could climb up a mountain with and discuss *The Grapes of Wrath* round the campfire later? Where were the ones who had read Thomas Mann and Marcel Proust? Climbing mountains now for Hamish and Don was a kind of nostalgia for their socialist past, and a homesickness for each other. Every time they reached a summit, and came across the summit cairn, it was like finding each other all over again.

Hamish and Don set out at seven in the morning as they had set out so many mornings on their weekend hikes. They lived for the weekends. They planned where they would go at the end of one trip so that they would have something to look forward to all week, to take the sore edge off that pining, bereft feeling at the end of a weekend. They liked the great outdoors, felt confined and restless indoors. Hamish worked for the council refuse department. He took the calls from people who had forgotten to put their bins out and needed to rearrange a special time for their bin, outside the normal collection day. They always sounded anxious and apologetic and told him a big story about why they'd forgotten to put it out in the first place as if he would only send the collection men out again if the excuse was good enough. You wouldn't believe the reasons people gave for forgetting their bin. Scottish people suffered a terrible guilt complex about not doing things they were supposed to do, Hamish believed, to the extent that it got quite ridiculous. 'My husband died in the middle of the night so I missed putting the bin out.'

Don worked as a hospital porter at the Royal Infirmary in Glasgow, that very dark building that looked from the outside as if it only ever welcomed the dying. Don had a bright smile on the wards and talked to all the patients as he took them for X-rays or to the operating theatre. Part of his job was to do the paper round in the morning too. He couldn't understand why so many patients got a tabloid. Some patients, jaundiced from cancer, could come out with quite shocking statements about asylum-seekers. Don would fall quite silent and wheel them to radiography. The thing that interested him was how many people kept bitter, rancorous ideas bubbling even when very seriously ill. You would think that dying would bring about some sort of elevated state where you would see a purer world just before you went, or something, Don thought.

Hamish and Don set out at seven on Saturday morning like they had done so many Saturday mornings before with their pieces and tablet and water and whisky, their sleeping bags rolled up and inside their rucksacks, in a snug sausage at the bottom, an extra pair of boxers apiece, spare socks, and a nylon climbing rope, just in case. Both men carried ice axes. What they liked about each other was that they were both manly-looking. Don liked Hamish's hairy chest. Don would have liked more hairs on his own chest. For some reason the only place he had a lot of hair was on his toes, the middle bit of his toes, running right across all of them. Both men were broad-shouldered, both greying or grey. Both had square, handsome faces. People mistook them for brothers, even, sometimes, twins, which was flattering for Hamish, given the difference of eight years between them. But they didn't look all that alike really. Maybe people thought they were related because they couldn't explain that particular closeness any other way. Maybe it was a visual thing, the way they stood quite closely together. Don was the more handsome of the two. For all the climbing and the walking, Hamish had quite a paunch on him now because, unlike Don, he was a sweet-tooth man and liked his puddings – rhubarb crumble, apple turnovers, lemon-meringue pie. He drew the line at chocolatey puddings, too rich, and felt that if he ate a fruit tart he was also eating something partly healthy. It was the thing Hamish missed most about his ex-wife, her puddings. She made the most excellent lemon-meringue pie. Relations between them were strained these days, Hamish wasn't likely to taste one like it ever again. Elspeth was now back from New Zealand and living in Dunfermline and probably the only satisfaction she got from life was knowing that Hamish would never taste her lemon-meringue pie as long as he lived. Hell mend him, Elspeth was probably thinking, separating the yolks from the whites, you make your bed, you lie on it.

Don liked a green olive or a bit of smelly cheese or natural yoghurt. He was much healthier than Hamish, had fish five times a week. He sprinkled bran on top of his herring to get his roughage. He drank plenty of water. He was starting to become acutely aware of time: time was galloping on a big horse and the only thing he could do to slow it down was eat his herring with his bran sprinkled on and walk his walks with his man. It was a brisk day with a bite in the air. They listened to the weather report and it said there might be fog later in the afternoon. But they had coped with fog before. They had both had a rough week. They needed the hills, the comfort of their shapes, the snap and crackle of the cold winter air, the crunch of the frozen earth under their feet, the stammer of the waterfall, the nonsense cries of birds. They never liked to change their plans once they had made them, to call things off – Hamish in particular. He liked to stick to what they had arranged or he got edgy and anxious, as if he might bring about some bad fortune by changing his plans at the last minute.

The morning air was damp and insinuated its way into their jackets. They drove their metallic-green

Volkswagen Polo to the parking spot beyond Loch Doine and left it there. They got out of the car and sniffed the air. Don was in a bit of a strange mood because one of his patients, who he had become very fond of, had just died. Although Don was used to this, getting close to people and them dying, it still hit him, it still made him think, By Christ I must live life to the full while I still can. Seeing the family arrive, go in and look at the body and say goodbye, pick up the small sad bag of belongings, turned his stomach every time. There was always someone who couldn't face looking. It had got so that Don could tell who that might be just by watching them come down the corridor.

If the fresh air could hit your lungs with force and you could take a long walk with a man you loved, if your legs were still working, and your heart was still pumping blood and you had your health, and you could get out, and you weren't stuck in a bed in a hospital, or stuck somewhere alone, scared, if you could find a quiet spot to take your man in your arms and kiss him, you weren't doing too bad, Don reckoned, especially because Hamish was a very good kisser. He'd start quietly, softly and then become more and more involved, till the whole kiss had a sweep to it, a peak, an intensity the likes of which Don had never known. He knew what expressions like *sweep you off your feet* meant now. Aye aye aye aye aye. Indeed, indeed, indeed. Both Don and Hamish disliked effeminate men.

Neither of them could ever fancy anybody effeminate. They liked real men like themselves, hard and rugged, with chunky cocks and broad shoulders and deep voices. They never asked themselves why this was. They just shook their heads and pulled faces when anybody too queenly or camp came into their lives. Some camp men were exceptionally witty, Don thought, but that was all there was to recommend them.

Although both men could drive, Don always did the driving. He opened the boot of the car and got the rucksacks out. It was lovely the way a car would just wait for you till when you returned, Don said. 'Well, it's no going to drive off on its own,' Hamish said and laughed. They liked sleeping the night out and then returning to the trusty wee car at the end of the long weekend. They had treated themselves to good-quality sleeping bags about five years ago because Don said, 'We expect sleeping bags to last forever but they don't really, they get thinner, sadder.' And Hamish laughed, a big, manly laugh, because he liked Don's turn of phrase. 'See you. See you,' Hamish said, and ruffled his hands through his lover's grey hair. Don's eyes lit up when he did this and a very bright, very boyish twinkle appeared, so that Hamish could imagine what he must have looked like when he was very wee. How, when anything pleased him extremely or excited him, his eyes would light in this way. A pure bright light, honestly bright as the star of Bethlehem if Hamish were religious. Or something.

Hamish and Don walked west along the track to Inverlochlarig, across a bridge and alongside the burn to join another track. It was now eight thirty in the morning. If the walk took them six hours, it would still be light enough when they finished. They followed the track north on the west bank of the burn. The ground was frozen under their feet. All of that was nae bother and they breathed in the fine cold air walking with one slightly in front of the other as if one was the other's shadow. The burn slithered in between the tight, snug mountains; something about burns made Hamish happy. They appeared like magic from the top of mountains and followed the strangest tracks all the way down. The two men walked in silence a lot of the time; and then suddenly one of them would start talking about something and they'd talk for another bit and then fall into silence again. After a bit the track ended and they followed a wide boulder-strewn beau-lach. It got a bit trickier. They started to climb. On their left, they could see the eastern crags of Stob Garbh. It was steeper than they'd thought. Don led and Hamish followed. Hamish got out of breath quicker and stopped more frequently on the small terraces after a particularly steep bank. They weren't talking at all now, just concentrating and enjoying pushing them-selves to extremes. It was icy, slippy. They needed to take extreme care, and now and then Hamish used his ice axe to cut steps out for himself. This was what was called an *entertaining ascent*, one that went on and on, with lots of little false promises of a summit, only to find that they still had yet further to go. There was nothing like the Scottish hills in winter, though, austere, with a flinty hardness. At twelve o'clock, still not having reached the double summit, or having yet seen the mirrored twins of Ben More and Stob Binnein, both men sat down to have their piece. This was maybe a mistake. Maybe they should have waited till they reached the summit. But Hamish was famished and exhausted and so they sat down on one of the small terraces. Hamish, out of puff, said, 'This is steeper than I was expecting.' And Don nodded. The fog was becoming a little more insistent, circling them, and their visibility was slightly impaired. Don said, 'Do you think we should call it a day?' Hamish said, 'Naw, we'll be all right. I want to see those mirrored twins.' 'We're no going to see much if this fog doesn't clear,' Don said. 'Och, it'll clear, it's that kind of mist that lifts. I wouldnie call it fog,' Hamish said, supping noisily from the flask of sugary tea. Don ate his ham piece and Hamish ate his jelly one because he wanted sweet. Hamish ate a banana too to give him more energy. 'Do you think we should rope up?' Don said. 'Naw,' Hamish said. 'We'll be fine.' They always took the rope with them and they seldom used it.

After a while, they set off again, refreshed from their wee break, climbing up and up and up until finally, at half-past twelve, they reached the summit. Time was slow when you were walking, strange and spacey. Ahead of them the steep north-east face of Cruach Adrain loomed. They took the narrow, winding path to reach the double summit. Don got there first and stood with his hands on his waist looking ahead. They had quite a clear view because the mist swirled below them. This high up was fairly clear. It was like being in an aeroplane above the clouds in a clear blue sky. What was the world like? If people just came out and walked up here every now and again, there would be less wars. Aye. Mountains made you and your petty struggles and the world and its crazy wars seem ridiculous. 'Argue with that,' Don said out loud, staring at the mountaintop. It was always worth pushing yourself that extra bit to get to the top. Nothing like it. Fucking nothing like it. There was the summit, covered in winter snow, standing firm and solid and implacable, loyal even. There was the mountain saying to Don, 'You've made it up to see me, son,' like a great old aunt with a sharp nose that always welcomes her nephews whilst simultaneously reprimanding them for not coming sooner. Don couldn't help himself: he always got a bit sentimental at a summit; he never lost that feeling of complete awe, amazed at what he was seeing. It was like the first time, all over again. He looked round to see Hamish struggle up the last bit, out of breath. He pulled him towards himself and held on to him. Hamish burrowed his head in Don's jacket for a minute or two before he looked around and took it all in. Don's eyes were wet. He kissed him. 'You daft sentimental bugger,' Hamish said, and kissed him again. He was out of breath so he couldn't give him a really long one. Not yet anyway.

They planned to save their tin of mince and tin of peas for supper. They never bothered with a compass. They thought compasses were for effeminate men. And they never bothered with maps either. Maps were for sissies. What you did when you were used to the walking climbing life was you followed your nose. You developed as keen a sense of direction as a dog and you took off in the full knowledge that you could always find your way back. And if for some reason you took a wrong turning you would be able to think of a number of different excuses for this, very plausible ones, just like the ones the people gave who had forgotten to put out their bins. You would say, 'Ah you see that threw me because that used to be that.' Or, 'Do you know what we did, when we got to that wee road down there we should have actually kept left.' Or, 'Seeing that huge heron was a big distraction by the way.' But anyhow, it was rare for Hamish or Don to get lost because they knew their country and it felt to them at least that their country knew them.

They loved their country as if it was just another way of loving each other. Even the weather, they took personally. If it was a fine day, they'd say, 'Look what's laid on for us today.' They loved the purple heather, the bleak moors, the staggering sweeps of the Highlands, the wide open beauty of the lowlands; the tight

winding road to Applecross, the youth hostel at Torri-
don, the road to Lochinver. They loved their lochs and
lochans, their fords and burns and streams, their cnocs
and corries and lagans, their creachanns and creags.
Even the word loch gladdened their hearts. In the
time of their love, they had walked round so many
lochs, they were drawn to the deep mystery of them,
Loch Ness, Loch Katrine, Lochearnhead, Loch Voil, Loch
Lomond, Loch Etive, Loch Fyne. Don might sometimes
stop and pick a bunch of heather and give it to Hamish,
laughing and pretending to be a little queenly in order
to get away with the gesture. 'Daarrrling, I thought
you might like this,' he would say using a Marlene
Dietrich accent. And Hamish would take it, laughing
away, slightly embarrassed but pleased as anything.
And they'd continue on. If one spotted a red deer, he
would tap the other on the arm and they'd both stand
rigidly still and watch the great red beauty of it sweep
their hills.

It was now one forty-five, that Saturday, and not a
particularly clear day. Never mind. Still always better
out than in and walking men can tend to get over-
obsessed with the weather and what it is doing or going
to do or not doing. Christ. A spot of rain, a bit of cold,
what was it to men like Hamish and Don.

They gathered themselves, because the fog was coming in thicker and faster. They followed the prominent
south ridge down to a gentle beaulach and continued
up easy slopes to the summit of Beinn Tulaichean. Don

said to Hamish, 'I think we should have turned back sooner, this fog is a bit of a worry.' Hamish said, 'All we've got to do now is go down along the ridge and watch out for that set of cliffs.' They started the descent. 'You can see where the expression rock solid comes from,' Hamish laughed gamely, gingerly putting one foot in front of the other, being careful of himself on the way down. The ice hid the shapes of things. It was slippery. There was always a bit of fear involved in a climb, always that feeling of having to take care of yourself, watch yourself. At last, at this part of his life, Hamish was in a relationship with somebody who he felt genuinely wanted to take care of him and who he wanted to take care of. It was safe, being with Don. Safe and trusty as the solid geology of the Highlands. He felt like he'd been with Don forever. He'd felt that even from the moment he met him; a kind of knowingness, that he'd never experienced before, a familiarity and an excitement, a huge excitement; at last finding somebody that spoke his language, at last finding a man with a big heart and a big mind that he could talk to about anything. Don was the kindest man Hamish knew, and the brightest. And the lovely thing was, he fancied him still, after these years together, his body still felt like he was coming home, every time. Every time Don took him and kissed him and bit his ear and rubbed his hairy chest and slowly traced his hand down his chest to his belly, Hamish would be already aroused, already hard, wanting him,

wanting him more than he'd ever wanted anybody.
'What are we like?' he would say after their sex to
Don. 'Have you ever had this before? No? Me neither.'
And then they'd sleep wrapped around each other
until they separated in the small hours, only to come
back together again in the morning. Don said once to
Hamish, and Hamish never forgot it, 'It's like your
body is a map and I am coming home.' Don had quite
a turn of phrase. Hamish laughed and teased him about
it, he said, 'Are you trying to be a poet or something?'
But he didn't forget it. It made him swell with pleasure,
feeling that loved, that desired.

Hamish felt like he had spent practically a lifetime
with the wrong people, with people that didn't quite
get him or appreciate him or ever truly know him. Yet
two weeks with Don, and Don could tell the tiniest
thing about him. If he was even slightly out of sorts,
Don would ask him if he was OK. He'd never known
the like. This is what people talk about, Hamish
thought to himself at the age of fifty-seven. This is
what people mean when they say they are in love, when
they talk of finding soulmates. 'Now I know what all
the fuss was about,' Hamish said and took Don's cock
in his mouth and sucked it till he came. Every part of
Don's body, he loved. He loved his flat stomach, how
hairless he was, he loved the shape of his cock, his
muscled legs and slightly knobbly knees, he loved the
flesh lobe of his ears. All of it. His whole body. He
had never before loved somebody's entire body like it

was his own. Even Don's feet and hands, especially his hands, he loved. He knew his body better than any he had ever slept with. Knew the puckered hole of his anus, the slap of his balls, knew how his cock felt soft and hard. Knew his tongue on the roof of his mouth. Knew the smell at the base of his neck, and the smell of his sweat under his arms. Though he was always very fresh, Don. It was a rare treat for Hamish to get to smell him properly. Don liked aftershave, but Hamish liked to smell somebody's real smell, without anything. Before they lived together, Hamish would like to know what Don was wearing so he could picture him. He'd never done anything as daft as that before either. It was a whole new world to him, the loved world with this particular man that felt so right for him, he was frightened anything might happen to part them. If they were flying, Hamish, normally terrified of flying, would be fine if he was holding Don's hand, because if the plane did crash it would take both of them, and he needn't worry about leaving him. They could go together. There was nobody he loved in that way and it was the same for Don. That was the other amazing thing about it. Usually it was unbalanced between people and one of the two had all the power. Not with him and Don. With him and Don the desire, the need, the love was just the same. The same the same, they'd say to each other and hold each other tight.

A mutual friend had introduced them seven years ago. That very first night in the pub, they couldn't stop talking. Don wrote his number down on the back of a beer mat that Hamish still has. Nothing happened the first night, but they arranged to meet. Hamish remembers going home that night and lying awake, knowing that he was on the edge of something, that he could fall off, that he could just lose it. There was something in Don that Hamish recognized in himself, a wildness, maybe even a narcissistic streak, a certain vanity. The next time they met, Hamish remembers thinking as he was shaving, let us take this slowly because this thing could be bigger than both of us. And half an hour later, not being able to stop themselves, just ripping off each other's shirts, pulling down the zips, so fast it was like devouring each other, like there was a wolf in them, a tiger, a storm. It wasn't soft and gentle like Hamish had imagined. It was rough, and for the first time ever Hamish took it as well as gave it. There was no Arthur and Martha, no divisions, they were both to each other, the same the same, mirrors. That first night they would end up in different parts of Don's living room without having a clue how they had got there. Sex for them both was like a fast story they were telling each other; it worked the way an imagination works, subconsciously, dangerously, subversively. There was no explaining it. The joy of finding each other's mouth, the hot taste of his lips, the rightness of his cock. They slept together well too, holding on to each other after the ravages, going in and out, it seemed of each other's dreams.

It was so much that after that first time, Don felt himself pull back a little. He could be consumed. They could burn each other out or drown or die. It was terrifying. What was it about it that terrified him? he asked himself, showering. Was it that he was afraid of it all falling apart? Was it that he feared losing himself to the extent that he merged with Hamish? Was it that he couldn't trust another human being that much? He had no quiet space in his head any more. Hamish took it all up. It was day and night and night and day, the first thing he thought about in the morning, the last thing at night. It was starting to feel obsessive. If he didn't hear from him, he worried that he was going to stop loving him. If he did hear from him, he worried he was going to consume him.

Don phoned Hamish one morning after they had seen each other nearly every day for two weeks and said, 'I think we are taking things a bit fast. It's making me panic. I need a bit of time to myself.' There was silence on the phone for a bit, then Hamish said, 'Fine with me. A good mate of mine wants to take me out tonight for dinner.' Don said, 'What mate?' 'I don't think I've told you about him. We used to have a thing going. But there's nothing now. So, you know, good pals.' Don put the phone down and caught sight of his face in the mirror. It looked bad. He spent that evening trying to watch the television and not even being able to take in what he was seeing. He felt sour and worried, and edgy. Nobody had ever made him feel like this before. The next day, he went round to Hamish's really early in the morning. Eight o'clock. Hamish was still in his pyjamas and looked all lovely and sleepy. Don pushed him against the wall of his hall and kissed him. 'I missed you,' he said. 'Don't be daft,' Hamish said. 'It was only one night.'

'Do you think maybe we should move in together?' Don asked Hamish after they had been together for one year. 'Naw,' Hamish said. 'It kills it. All that domestic shite. You'd get annoyed with me for not making the bed, or washing the dishes, or you know. You're tidier than me. You're always tidying up even when you come here.'

'I just like a bit of order,' Don said a touch defensively. 'See? Before we knew where we were we would have destroyed the passion. Come here.'

'Do you remember that time you didn't want us to live together,' Don shouted going down the side of the mountain.

'No!' Hamish shouted. 'I always wanted us to live together. It was you who wasn't sure.'

'It was not!' Don shouted. 'You've got a terrible memory.'

The fog was really dense now, you could cut it with an ice axe. Both men climbed down into it. Slabs and slabs of fog. It was cold on their faces, wet, damp. Hamish was behind Don; momentarily, he had let him out of his sight. He started to panic; he couldn't see Don. 'Let's just get down,' he shouted. He was feeling a little breathless, and light-headed. A little odd. He wasn't sure quite what was the matter with him. He didn't want to mention anything to Don because he was a bit of a worrier, Don. He knew all the things that could go wrong with people, working in the Infirmary, and he knew that the line between life and death was sharp and thin, like the sharp edge of the mountain. But Don being Don sensed something, maybe something in his voice, and shouted, 'Are you all right? Do you think we should rope up? I'll come back up and you go first then I can keep an eye on you.'

Don turned round and started climbing back towards Hamish and lost his footing. The rocks under him scrambled and gave way to him and he felt himself slide and slip and tumble a good way down the mountain in slow motion. His body gathered a momentum all of its own and some part of Don's brain detached itself for a slow moment and said, 'Look at what is happening to me, I am falling,' and then another part said very quickly, 'It's coming for me.' For the smallest of moments, Don was outside himself and in, the watcher and the watched. In the gap between falling and falling again, Don was both of them, he was Hamish too; he was everything they ever had been. He was all of their lovers. He was all of their mistakes. Look at what is happening to me, Hamish, I am going down, he thought as he tumbled and hit the sharp edge of a cliff. And finally he stopped tumbling and lost consciousness. There was silence then, a slow stopping of things, a soft snowy, downy, feathery silence that held open its soft skin hands and let him rest. Like the faithful stones that made up a cairn, a marking of things. A comforting silence that took him in and continued whatever it was doing on its own.

Hamish could not see where Don had gone. He heard him shout out, then he heard him fall; he heard the rocks come apart and give way. A scrambling and a stuttering of stones and rocks. He followed as fast as he could in the direction of the sounds, taking care not to slip himself. One step in front of the other. One boot here and another here and another here. He stopped as he saw Don's ice axe at his foot. He picked it up because they might need it. He tried to call for help but his mobile had no reception. He shouted Don's name over and over again. 'Don! Don! Don!'

The inside of his mouth was completely dry. He could barely swallow. He can't have gone that far. He can't have fallen that far, he told himself. Be sensible. It's not like fucking Mount Everest. It's not even the Cairngorms. It's a slip. He's slipped and I will find him in a second and he is going to be all right. It's a slip, that's all. Plenty people slip. Experienced climbers slip for fuck sake. For fuck sake.

The fog was like a herd of cattle now, coming towards him in shapes, slobbering at his face, advancing. There was no escaping it. If they had turned back. If they had stayed in. If they had not wanted to see the mirrored twins. If they had done this climb in the summer. If they had never met. The line between what happens and what could happen is really very fine.

Hamish was down on his knees now, patting the mountainside for Don, feeling his way, feeling the shapes of the hills like he would stroke Don's body, the dips and the crevices. He might have missed him. If he fell from somewhere just behind him, and fell in that direction he would be over there. He searched the ground below that point, feeling with his hands, groping the ground. He was frantic now. He tried his phone again. Still no fucking reception. Time hadn't stopped. Time was advancing. If Don was hurt; if Don was badly hurt, this time was costing him. This was time Don needed. If he was bleeding. Hamish could feel he was hurt. He could feel it because he was so linked to him, so close to him. He could feel he was seriously hurt like twins can feel each other is hurt. He could feel his need.

Hamish stopped for a second and listened. Was that breathing he could hear? Could he hear Don calling him? He listened again. He remembered Don saying, early in their relationship, 'Love will find a way.' He repeated this sentence to himself like a person in need of psychological assistance. He willed himself to find him. He cleared his head of every thought. He stopped trying to work out rationally where he would have fallen, as if a falling body was a mathematical equation. He cleared his head and as he cleared his head the fog started to lift a little, just as mysteriously as it had descended. The white fingers of the fog stroked his cheeks. He looked at his watch. He had been missing Don for half an hour. It felt like days. He stood staring at his watch. He would let five minutes go. He would watch both hands on his clock face go round until five minutes were up and then he would find Don. In those five minutes the fog would vanish completely to the strange, mysterious, silent place it came from. In those five minutes Don would regain consciousness because he must be unconscious because otherwise he would have shouted him. Hamish took a deep breath. His heart was beating so fast, he could feel the throb and the pulse of it. He took another deep breath. He must stay calm for five minutes. At the end of those five minutes he would rescue his lover and they would be fine, really, they would both be fine and they would be telling their pals about this soon. This would be a story. Hamish had to wait for five minutes precisely; then this could be a story. This could be a story that they would dine out on for months. Months and months and months. He would let Don tell his part, how they saw the mirrored twins, how happy they'd been and then how they had started to descend. And then Hamish would take over; Hamish would take over the telling of the story. How long he'd searched for. What was in his mind. He could hear himself telling his friends, slurping on a big glass of red wine, 'I was, like, frantic. I was totally out of my mind. But I knew I was

going to find him. I knew that I was going to find him.
Because, look at it this way. I couldn't not. Do you
know what I'm saying? I couldn't not find him. There
was no way I was leaving the side of the mountain.
When the rescue men came, I was already lying by
Don, holding his head in my lap, kissing him, kissing
him, putting oxygen in his lungs. I'd already got a
reaction from him.' 'I always react to your kisses,'
Don would be saying to big dirty laughs from their gay
friends.

When five minutes were up precisely, the fog had
more or less cleared. Hamish opened his rucksack and
took one of the red apples out and placed it where he
was standing. He walked in a straight line in what he
imagined to be south of the red apple. No Don. He
placed the tin of mince in that spot then walked west
from the tin of mince. Still no Don. He put the tin of
peas down and walked north from the tin of peas.
He marked each spot with his memory, so that he
wouldn't keep repeating the same ground, over and
over. He would find Don before he had to leave the can
of McEwan's. He thought of the mountains, the mirrored twins, how they stood a certain distance apart,
almost opposite each other. He walked back to the tin
of peas and decided to walk due south-east. He tried
the reception on his phone. Then he thought of send-
ing a text. Sometimes text worked where calls didn't.
He sent an SOS text to his best pal, Charlie. He told
Charlie roughly where they were. He said Don has

fallen. Lost. Need ambulance. Rescue. He walked due south-east from the tin of peas and there in the distance was something, a shape of somebody. First he noticed the blue waterproof coat, huddled into the hillside. Then he noticed that he was lying in a strange distorted position, like no position he had ever seen him in, with one leg splayed out in an odd direction. He couldn't see his face. He was turned away from him. He rushed towards him, full of a dread that stopped him in his tracks for a couple of terrible thick seconds. Then he went into overdrive. He took extreme care of himself as he went towards Don as fast as he could without falling himself. He found a frozen grassy slope and headed towards him. Hamish could barely breathe. There in a heap with a broken bone protruding from his leg was Don. He was still breathing. There was a lot of blood. Hamish unravelled the ties around the sleeping bag. He made Don a makeshift splint, putting the ice axe against his leg and wrapping the sleeping-bag strings around and around it as tight as he could. He made sure the sharp end of the ice axe was facing away from Hamish's leg. There was nothing else he could use. There were no sticks. He knew he had to try and stop the flow of blood. Then he knew he had to keep him warm. He placed Don's broken leg inside the bottom of the sleeping bag, trying not to disturb his leg. You weren't supposed to move people at all, Hamish knew that. But needs must. He tried not to look at the bone, but somehow he kept seeing flashes of it even when he wasn't looking; the whiteness of the bone shocked him. He wished it was him lying there, not Don. Don would be better at this bit. He wished he had an empty black plastic bin bag to put the leg in first. He rubbed some whisky on Don's lips, and Don's eyes fluttered open. Hamish said, 'You're going to be all right, my love. You're going to pull through this. Do you know how much I love you, do you?' He kissed Don's cheeks.

Don was in so much pain he couldn't feel anything at first; and then it started coming in, a huge throbbing fire to his leg. It felt as if Hamish was squeezing his leg right through. It felt as if Hamish was right in there stroking his bone. Don was lying at a strange angle to himself. He looked up to the sky. He noticed that the sky was drained of all colour. Strange, swirling moments passed. He noticed the clouds in the sky were ash-grey, brooding. Somebody was holding his hand; somebody kind was holding his hand. He went away for a bit and came back again. Time seemed very, very slow. He remembered falling. That was very slow too. The moment when he said to himself he was done for was startling, lucid. Then there was a void. Nothingness. And now, little flecks of something, dots and spinning spots and somebody holding his hand. Way, way in the distance, over the other side of the mountain, Don could hear Hamish say, 'Do you know how much I love you, do you?' Like an echo. Was it an echo or was it his real voice? And were they birds that were flying from Hamish's head or were they thoughts? Was that Hamish again thinking exactly the same thing at the same time in the same moment? The twin mountains huddled them in close, closer than secrets. It was late afternoon by this time, and the dark was coming down on them. If they weren't found soon, they might not make it. Don was thinking that maybe the mirrored twins had claimed them, taken them in. Hamish was thinking the same thing. Hamish carefully untied the rucksack on Don's back. Maybe it had cushioned some of the fall, maybe it would have been worse if he hadn't had it on. He pulled the other sleeping bag out of the rucksack and climbed into it. He put Don's head on his lap. It was very cold now. Don's teeth chattered against his will. Maybe it was the pain. It was only a matter of time. He checked his phone again. There was a message in his inbox from Charlie. It said, Keep calm. Am on to it. In less than the time it would take them to tell this story; in less than the time it took that first night to have that drink together; in less than the time it took to answer a morning's refuse calls; help would arrive with its spinning wings and airlift them out of here.

Time passed more slowly than ever, and the dark started its long descent into night. There was only an inch of light left in the sky. Hamish scrambled in Don's rucksack for the box of matches. There was a full box. They weren't damp. Don moaned; he cried out in a voice Hamish hardly recognized, a voice distorted by pain. Hamish stroked his loved head. Hamish said, 'We are getting through this. There's absolutely no way we are not going to live to tell this story.'

picador.com

blog
videos
interviews
extracts